BODYSURFING

A Catherine Kint Mystery

HUGH MCGINLAY

STORY BY

Hugh McGinlay

Louise Kent

Adam Palmer

Clan Destine
PRESS

First published by Clan Destine Press in 2021

Clan Destine Press
PO Box 121, Bittern
Victoria, 3918 Australia

National Library of Australia Cataloguing-In-Publication data:

McGinlay, Hugh

Bodysurfing

ISBN: 978-0-6450021-4-0 (paperback)
ISBN: 978-0-6450426-1-0 (eBook)

Cover Design by © Willsin Rowe
Design & Typesetting by Clan Destine Press

Clan Destine
P R E S S

www.clandestinepress.net

To Andrea and Hugh –
who showed me the beach, kept me safe, listened to my stories.

1

Some people just move fast. It's spectacular, but you know you're waiting for the crash.

~ Yvonne McSweeney

The question was: what time is acceptable to have one's first drink? This led to the second question: if time is meaningless on holiday, does that render the first question moot?

Catherine Kint was corporeally placed at the 11th beach, Ocean Grove, Australia. A town you could call sleepy for ten months of the year and a swarming hive of holiday makers for the hottest two. She had the sun on her back, sand in her toes, a towel under her and gin in her very near future. As moments in life went, this was above passable.

She turned her head to face her holiday companion. Detective Britt Houden was sitting up on her towel and studiously reading a novel of throw-away detective fiction. Britt was using an Australian Labor Party candidate's political flyer as a bookmark. Flyers had been thrust upon them yesterday. Bookmark aside, Britt seemed intent on not letting anything – wind, by-election or climate change – distract her from her holiday. Her whole self was concentrated on the book. You could have taken her picture as an example of "busy person intent on unwinding, thanks".

'The time for refreshments is surely at hand.'

Britt didn't look up from her page. 'Do you even know what the time is?'

'No, I'm off clock this week.'

'Does that stop time, or health, or logic?'

'I'm stepping outside logic and the trappings of convention into a place called "holiday". There's a beach and a quaint town full of people trying desperately to make sense of life. I have decided the answer will descend upon me quicker if I give over to the calm chaos of the universe from this sandy vantage point. I've been here for three days. It's wonderful.'

Britt's mouth twitched, which Catherine saw as a moral victory.

Britt had begun each day of their sabbatical – Britt's from Homicide Squad, Catherine's from the rigours of millinery – with a 45-minute run along the beach. Britt's exercise routine was resuming after a six-month hiatus due to a broken ankle, that last week had been pronounced healed. After the run, Britt would finish the newspaper and her macrobiotic breakfast before Catherine dragged herself to the couch of their holiday home for her morning's contemplation of the day. Britt then made coffee in the kitchenette: her first and only of the day; Catherine's first of the four that hour.

Of course, not even Britt could remain focused all the time. Last night she'd even belted out a fabulous version of *Flame Trees* at the local karaoke club, after some subtle persuasion and unsubtle cocktails. The memory pleased Catherine, who saw it as a civic duty to continue this fine detective's unwinding.

Which lead back to the current conundrum of when to have a gin: should she start too early, Britt would think it improper. She might even decide to have an alcohol-free night or something equally unsavoury.

Catherine heard the cries of seagulls and smelled salt on the wind. Compared to the main street's yearly summer overpopulation, the beach was idyllic. Of course it brought the crowds, but no one complained on the beach. Families were playing, children squealed happily in the foam and people reclined at various places in the sand. Catherine's view was broken by the form of a large haggard man in a dark flannel shirt staring out to sea as he carried a piece of driftwood in both arms. He looked towards Catherine and adjusted his glasses awkwardly before moving on. Catherine again thought of gin and glanced sidelong at Britt, knowing that she would never have worried about asking her usual offsider, Boris.

That did it: pleasure should not be thought about, but experienced. She was just about to reach for the esky when the screaming started.

At first, Catherine thought it was a shark attack. The initial screamer was a young mother, about 33 metres away, reaching out for a stunned boy in red speedos. Catherine looked past him in the water for a fin, but instead saw the limp body rolling in with the waves.

Britt was already racing; already halfway between their vantage point and the surf. The body was being pulled in by two men, an arm each side. The way its torso hung gave Catherine little hope for resuscitation. Also, the fact that the body was clothed in what looked like jeans and a pale blue shirt indicated this was not a swimmer.

The two burly men reached the shore and dropped the body gently a few metres from the waterline. Quickly, there were two dozen people, staring.

Britt took charge. 'Back everyone, please. I'm Police.' Catherine only then registered that Britt's one-piece bathers were navy blue, and probably standard uniform.

Catherine joined in the crowd control. 'Back please. She's police.'

The body was male, about 170 centimetres and very, very dead.

Even as Catherine elbowed past the final layers of gawkers, Britt did not drop to begin CPR but kneeled, very carefully. From the way the body was slumped, Catherine guessed he'd been dead for some hours.

'Could someone call 000, please?' Britt's voice rang out; it wasn't a question.

Catherine saw that Britt was suddenly more relaxed than she had been for the past 72 hours. Then she was drawn back to the body, into noticing other things: the paleness of the skin; the salt build-up in the hair; the lack of obvious defence wounds – but she knew they could be subtle. Some part of her brain knew that the wind had changed, and she should be feeling cold, but wasn't.

One of the men who'd brought the body in – an older man with a white beard and a towel around his waist – pushed through the crowd, a phone to his ear. 'I've got Police on the line now. They want to know if they should send an ambulance, too.' Unlike many in the crowd, he wasn't shaking

'Yes, send one.'

The man conveyed the message down the line.

Britt's whole stance declared she was a cop as effectively as a badge on her bathers would have. When a golden retriever came too close, she said, 'Pull your dog back' and was obeyed.

Catherine took a good look at the dead man, her eyes going "soft" –

open and relaxed, taking in everything without prejudice. It was a useful approach, when she didn't know what she was looking for.

The man was face up, his soft features bloated by the time in the water. He'd probably been good looking in life. He wore a pale blue business shirt and black trousers, not jeans. One shoe was missing, exposing a grey sock. The salt stains on the trousers were becoming more obvious as the wind dried the material. There was some soiling around the waist. His belt buckle looked expensive. His nails were manicured.

'The shirt would have been too hot for during the day, even with this wind,' Catherine said.

Britt nodded. 'Yep, he wore these clothes out last night.'

Catherine followed Britt's gaze out to the waves. 'What are you looking at?'

'How the tide is coming. I want to guess where he may have drifted from.'

'The tide's starting back in. If his body was on the beach in the early morning he could have come from anywhere.'

'I think I can narrow it down.'

'You're not on holiday any more, are you?'

The sun broke through cloud as Britt smiled grimly. 'Give a girl a minute, Catherine.'

They were interrupted by the police sirens in the distance. In the three minutes it took for the uniforms to arrive, Britt told three people to heel their dogs and four people not to take photos.

Two uniforms got out of the police car. The blue and red lights were vivid in the now overcast conditions. A dark-haired woman was with them first, though Catherine was taken by her partner, a tall Asian man who walked more slowly. He was taking in the whole scene. Soft eyes. Some people did it instinctively.

'Move back please, Miss.' The female cop took Britt's position at the body's side. Britt grimaced, but went back to scanning the sea.

'You're police,' the male cop said to Britt.

'Detective Britt Houden, Homicide.' Britt offered a hand.

'Constable Duc Nguyen. This is Senior Constable De Carle.' His face flickered. 'Always hard when work follows you on holiday.' De Carle raised a manicured eyebrow and returned to crowd control.

Britt suppressed a grin. 'It might be a drowning, but the clothing suggests otherwise.'

'Yep, he's not a solo angler in that outfit.'

'No, he wasn't in the sea deliberately. Have there been any mayday calls from boats about people overboard?'

Nguyen looked at his partner, who shook her head.

Catherine cleared her throat. Britt motioned with her hand, an afterthought. 'This is Catherine.'

'You're homicide too?' Nguyen asked.

'Millinery.'

He was deadpan. 'Must be a new division.'

From down the beach came another siren. The ambulance was coming in. Nguyen pulled on a pair of blue nitrile gloves. Catherine suppressed a smile as he passed a pair to Britt.

'Look at this, Detective.' He pointed to the discolouration at the lower left side of the body's torso.

'Perhaps we should wait for the suits,' suggested Britt.

Catherine thought she heard Duc's partner grunt.

'Homicide's already here,' Nguyen said. 'Let's just check.'

They lifted the body slightly; Britt pulled up the shirt, revealing a puncture wound, three centimetres across. It had rough edges, with a Y shape tapering towards his upper body. As stab wounds went, this was ugly.

'There's always a job to do, Detective.' Nguyen said quietly.

'Yep, more to this than a drowning. Let's check his pockets and book the lab.' Britt was definitely no longer on holiday.

'You should call the suits now, Duc,' Catherine spoke over the body.

Duc and Britt's faces came up in tandem, quickly. Catherine kept hers blank. 'You're wearing bathers, Britt,' she said. 'It's an odd look.'

Britt's eyes flickered, and she nodded slightly. 'You're right. Call homicide, Nguyen. We need to leave this to them.'

The ambos were talking to De Carle. Nguyen got on the phone to homicide.

Catherine and Britt knew they were supposed to walk away now, but neither did. Britt's eyes hadn't moved from the body, while Catherine watched Nguyen on his phone. She had only just met him, but she thought he seemed frustrated by what he was hearing. After another minute, he approached them, his smile more of a grimace. 'Thanks Detective, you can go back to your holiday now.'

Britt wasn't done yet. 'Who's coming from homicide?'

'I don't know. I've been told to take photos and organise the ambos.'

Britt stiffened. 'Photos?'

Catherine knew that had Britt been given the case, there would have been a ring of Police tape around the scene until she arrived, so she could look at it as it has been found. Photos were never an adequate option: you couldn't smell them or hear them, or see who was watching.

Britt closed her eyes, clearly reminding herself that for the next two weeks she was trying to leave behind her reputation as a stickler for protocol. Part of the protocol was that you don't mess with other people's investigations.

De Carle was watching Britt closely.

Duc spoke quietly enough that De Carle wouldn't hear. 'You should go. I'm outranked and you're on holiday.'

'Right,' Britt said loudly after a second. 'I'll do that.'

De Carle's smile of triumph was evident to Catherine, as was his ignoring it. The onlookers stared at Britt and Catherine as they walked back to their beach towels and their briefly suspended holiday.

They had little to consider aside from mortality. Catherine exhaled and looked out to sea. The beach was a good place to be at such times, but it wasn't as good as being busy.

Catherine knew from experience in her former life in CSI that her thoughts would be linear and mournful for the next while, as they were anytime she saw a body. As people from the beach moved past, alone, or in groups, she knew death was changing their thoughts too. Everyone's time was limited: a good thing to be reminded of, even on holiday.

Fifty minutes later, the ambulance drove off towards the surf beach, where it would get back to the road. De Carle took three more photos of the sand where the body had been – for what reason, Catherine couldn't think, and judging by Britt's face, neither could she. Nguyen gave Britt a nod as they left, his high cheekbones rising in a little smile. Catherine watched the cops walk back towards the carpark and enjoyed the miffed silence she was sharing with Britt.

'Poor fella.' Britt broke into Catherine's thoughts.

'Yeah, that wound was unusual.'

Britt smiled wryly.

'What?'

'We met in fashion week, didn't we?'

'Eight years ago. You wore one of my hats.'

'Nobody else from Fashion Week would describe a jagged stab wound as "unusual".' She pulled at her nose. 'I can't believe you had to go all Detective Sergeant Williams on me back there.'

Catherine sucked at her lip. She'd wondered if this would be mentioned. 'Someone had to. You were back at work, practically in your underwear.'

Britt pulled at the shoulder strap of her bathers. 'Yes. It was like one of those "being at work in your underwear" dreams. Thanks for saying it.'

'Thanks for hearing it. I hate it when my boss gets mentioned.'

'Probably why you haven't had one for years.' Just as she spoke, the sun returned from behind a cloud and Catherine enjoyed the warm presence of its light on her back. The day was looking up.

'Crack that esky, Kint. I need a drink.'

'Oh, now that, Detective, is a great idea.'

2

They can all tell me not to be angry, but it's the only thing that's kept me safe.
They never understand that, until it's too late.
~ Travis Barker

Four hours later, Catherine was drinking in both the ambience of the Zebra bar – one of Ocean Grove's three nightspots and the closest to their lodgings – and the wonder of the lemon rind freshness of her gin. It being 7.20 in the evening, the refills has slowed, but Catherine was feeling buoyant; so it seemed was Britt, who bopped as she brought another round to the table.

A fifteen-strong group was drinking on the balcony. Britt and Catherine had surmised they were connected to the discovery of the dead man: they were drinking hard and taking turns to cry. Some wore malachite green tee shirts, which Catherine thought odd for a bunch of not-so-merry men and women. Another one was crying now, so Britt brought her bopping down a touch.

Catherine caught the vibe and kept her voice low. 'I swear your mood improved as soon as you saw a case you didn't have to solve.'

Britt kept quietly bopping to the Jackson 5 song that was throbbing through the speakers. 'It's entirely possible. Though maybe the seventy two hours we've been here is the correct amount of time it takes a busy person to unwind.'

Catherine wondered how her friend would look at forty. 'Have you ever thought about slowing down?'

Britt's eyes flashed. 'Did my mother put you up to this?'

Catherine snorted into her drink. 'No, I will never do that to you and I expect the same in return. Let's broaden it to homicide in general. You have 80 per cent of professionals who work 50 plus hours each week and continually burn the candle at both ends. My question: is there a better way?'

Britt rubbed her nose. 'Short answer: Yes. Longer answer: Yes, but more crooks will get away. The logistics of having two detectives sharing a case is too much. By the time you'd debriefed on what happened on your colleagues' days off, you've significantly cut down investigation time. You could have more beat cops doing shorter shifts I guess, but some jobs take all the hours you can give them.'

'Yep. That's what I thought you'd say.'

'I'm sure there are milliners who work long hours.'

'Every hour I work is long. That's why I do so few.'

Britt nodded, acknowledging the above par quip for this time of evening. 'I think anyone, cop, milliner or truckie, could find ways to work less. It just involves more reprogramming of the brain than I care to tinker with. Then, there's the other thing.'

'What's that?'

'The system. I tell Williams I want to go part time and he'll have me off homicide quicker than you can scream glass ceiling. It's not even because he's a prick. He's not.'

'You say.'

'So do you, at times. But it's not even because he's a prick. It's because he's him. He's part of the system.'

Catherine sighed.

Britt smiled. 'Buck up. You're starting a very cool revolution by slowing down. Revolutions that don't kill half the population take time.'

'Maybe if we worked on it harder?'

'Now you're getting it. Hot chips?'

'Perfect.'

Their revelry was interrupted by a ruckus from the other side of the bar. A large man was standing and berating the man he'd been drinking with.

'He was nothing. Just a smartarse fag. Don't get uppity on me.'

The screamer had a tattoo of a swallow on his neck and his menacing bulk made you want to be far from him. The man on the receiving end was smaller, but he was relaxed, which seemed unnatural when being verbally beaten by someone so much bigger. Catherine noticed a subtle cracking of the screamer's tattooed knuckles. Someone at the balcony table stood up, but sat down again quickly.

The tattooed man continued his tirade, getting louder. 'And don't start that shit about the cause. We're under attack, every day, and it's just about money to some.' The other man was motionless but uncowed. When he spoke, the words didn't carry.

Suddenly, the large man was struck dumb. He turned on his heel and marched towards the stairs leading to the street.

'Barker!' the small man called out.

The big man, Barker, slowed, then pushed on down the stairs.

The smaller man rubbed the side of his rattish face and sculled the last of his pot of beer. Then he followed the man out.

'Hey, look down there,' Britt drew Catherine's attention to the view of the main drag through the pub's windows.

The street was mostly empty, with a few teenagers visible outside the hamburger joint. Barker, the man who had been yelling, walked towards the west side, his bulk filling the footpath. Two familiar cops approached him – Nguyen and De Carle, from the beach. They must have been clocking up the overtime in tourist season.

Nguyen called out to Barker as they got closer. He was too far away to hear. Barker did not stop, almost pushing De Carle out of the way. Catherine heard Britt's intake of breath as De Carle's hand went to her sidearm. Nguyen touched her shoulder and called something out to Barker, who slowed and then stopped.

Nguyen walked towards him slowly, his hands relaxed, De Carle hanging back.

Barker's shoulder slumped, then he half-reared, before catching himself and returning to his normal hulk. He was a full head taller than the poised Nguyen, whose hands were still at his hips, not touching his weapon. He gestured to the waiting car. Barker slowly shook his head and then moved towards it.

Only then did Catherine realise she'd been holding her breath.

As Barker got into the back of the car, there was a small round of applause, which the cops either didn't hear or ignored.

They drove away without sirens.

Britt took a long sip. 'That one has a cool head.'

Catherine leaned back in her seat. 'With a lovely face on it, too.'

Britt raised an eyebrow. 'Didn't think you'd noticed.'

'Oh, we're not quite at the sharing rubber glove stage, but I notice things.' She shifted her leg to avoid the kick Britt directed under the table and went to the bar to order the hot chips.

Hours later – they wouldn't be able to say whose idea it was – one had run towards the water and the other had followed. One minute they were walking towards their beach house and the next they were half-naked, splashing into the ocean. Whether it was the alcohol, the long day, or the knowledge that they had found one person dead and seen another lose their liberty in the past twenty-four hours, didn't matter.

Britt was laughing as her feet were submerged to the ankles, warm, even though it was the middle of the night. Catherine slowed as the water came to her waist, calling out to Britt and hearing her friend yell back.

A wave crashed against her chest, warm and harsh. Catherine tasted the salt and thought momentarily of sharks. Let them come, she thought, they can't take all of us.

Britt was singing again, off-key and beautiful. Catherine began treading water. Something small, but definitely alive, touched her foot and she shuddered. Instinct returned and she pulled back towards shore, relieved to feel sand underneath her toes. Britt was further off, to her left and closer to the shore. Smart cookie, that cop. No drowning for her. Catherine thought of the common term used in emergency rooms – PFO – Pissed, Fell Over – and wondered if there was a drowning equivalent. She thought again about the dead man's body rolling fully clothed through the same waves hours earlier.

Britt had stopped singing. Catherine could see her silhouette in the moonlight, water up to her waist; watching the stars. Probably thinking similar thoughts.

At first, Catherine thought the sound was a gull; high pitched but throttled somehow. Then it came again. Not a gull; gulls didn't cry. Not like that. It was the unmistakable sound of someone sobbing as they walked along the beach.

Catherine looked at Britt, still focused on the celestials above. Catherine moved towards the beach, suddenly aware of her nakedness and her scattered clothes. The crier moved past; she sounded young. Catherine reached the shore and heard the sound again, behind her.

'Are you all right?' She called into the darkness as she found her tee shirt and Britt's jeans – which would have come up to Catherine's chest.

'What?' Britt's voice from the water.

'Not you, dear.'

'Is someone out there?'

Catherine paused. The sound was muffled now, almost out of earshot. 'There was, gone now.'

Then a matriarchal voice briefly filled the beach, calling out a name: 'Kayla!'

Catherine pulled on her – now found– shorts and looked up. The shout came from the direction into which the cries had disappeared. Not the same voice. If the crier had been a flute, this voice was a bugle, or a gong.

Britt came out of the water; Catherine passed Britt her shirt.

'Thanks. Did you hear that shout?' asked Britt.

'Couldn't miss it. Someone walked past before, crying.'

'I didn't hear that.' Britt snorted. 'Ah, look at this. My wallet is still in my bag. Yet they say the town is full of thieves. Don't know much, these folk.'

Catherine smiled. The water and the crying girl had pushed her back into sobriety, or an approximation. It seemed Britt was not similarly afflicted.

They walked, slowly and wet, towards home. Britt started singing again.

Four hours later, Catherine lay awake. It happened sometimes. She couldn't stop thinking about voices on the beach, about lonely people crying. Hats, the pitfalls of hedonism and dead lovers also came up in the slurring chatter of her 5am brain.

This was the time Britt usually got up: perhaps they had been reversed in the past twenty four hours? Perhaps Catherine should go jogging.

No, body, no, she whispered. Such thoughts are tricks murmured by not sober minds. The body wants desperately to feel better, but doesn't know how poorly these lungs will feel 500 paces down the beach.

Sleep wasn't coming anytime soon, however. Catherine tried to enjoy the mattress under her, the doona that covered her, too warm. She tried to be conscious of the whole experience of the moment, and went back to the pitfalls of hedonism. Being one with the moment didn't erase the fact that 5am Catherine absolutely resented 5pm Catherine's choices – which had squeezed every jolt of moisture out of her and left her smoked.

That said, there had been plenty of times when it was 5am Catherine making the poor choices, and so the duality of her evening and dawn selves were capable of trading the halo for horns at any given day.

The darkness was lifting. Catherine could hear birds chirping. Not the warbles of city birds, but the early coos that would morph into the bayside squawks of gulls. Catherine decided that being on holiday meant she could get up whenever she wanted, even at a time that wouldn't usually appeal.

Catherine opened her bedroom door onto the shared corridor. Light crept in and illuminated the grey carpet, worn down by years of sandy feet. She heard a bump and thought Britt might be preparing for her morning run. She cocked her head. The noise didn't repeat. Catherine waited and heard a sound she'd never heard before: gentle, almost cartoonish snoring, coming from Britt's room.

Catherine grinned.

The street was quiet, except for the faint crash of waves. The morning was warm, a harbinger of the heat that would arrive with a vengeance later. Catherine walked towards the town, wondering what day it was. One of the great holiday pleasures was the way time didn't so much stand still as simply cease being relevant. Somewhere, people would be saying things like, 'Not bad for a Tuesday.' It made her present moment all the better that she was far away from those people.

Almost every electricity pole bore a poster for a political party. The by-election was four weeks away, but the campaign was in full swing, even if the town was mostly full of tourists who were ineligible to vote locally. Through her foggy morning vision, Catherine compared the three posters, spruiking the candidate of the three major parties: Liberal, Labor and Greens. Three white faces, two women and a man, all smiling sagely as if they had the keys to the universal cabinet of wisdom.

Sometimes our body tells us something is wrong before our brain can catch up, and for a couple of seconds, Catherine had no idea why she had stopped moving. Then she saw three Greens posters in row, all of the same face, above the words: "Brandon Miles-Barclay – a new voice bringing South Barwon forward".

Catherine had assumed the Greens would not be a favourite in South Barwon, but she knew with certainty that Brandon Miles-Barclay would not be its new voice. This was the same face she had seen on a dead man, less than 24 hours earlier.

Catherine shivered. More sleep would perhaps have been the better option.

The traffic noticeably worsened as she got closer to town. She saw three cars and even a motorbike. She could understand why the locals hated this time of year, which had been a regularly overheard topic of conversation in the past week.

Town itself was waking up. The main drag smelled of the fresh bread being unloaded from ovens in the bakery, mixing with the overripe dustbins, still full from the previous night. A teenager in a collared shirt was unlocking the supermarket, and a woman tied back her dreadlocks before taking the chairs off the table at a café.

On the street, one person stood out, her stillness in stark contrast to the industry of these other people. The young girl sat on a bench on the side of the mall, facing outwards and staring glassily down the street, seeing nothing. As the sun rose on her left, her profile was illuminated almost to the point of a halo. Catherine, intrigued, moved to avoid the glare. The girl's eyes didn't follow her.

She was in her mid-teens, mousy brown hair dyed red in places. She wore the vaguely gothic fashion of the day – which made Catherine aware of (a) how ridiculous fashion was and (b) how she would never have thought such a thing when younger. Age was creeping up on her. Unseasonably, the girl wore a warm jacket loosely over her clothes. She had a small duffle bag beside her.

The girl didn't register Catherine as she came closer. Judging by her skin, eyes and hair, Catherine decided the girl was not in an altered state, only tired.

Catherine, wondering if yesterday's boozing was affecting her judgement, made a snap deduction.

'Kayla?'

The girl's eyes darted and met Catherine's. They blinked, trying to place her. Her eyebrows knitted.

'Who the hell are you?' Her voice was high.

'I'm Catherine. Are you all right?'

'Are you a social worker?'

'No.' Catherine shrugged, looking down at herself. 'I'm Catherine. I make hats.'

'How do you know me?'

'I don't. But I know someone called Kayla had a rough night and you look like you had a rough night. Can I sit down?'

Kayla stared at Catherine. She had a sleeper earing in her nose, which with the faded dye in her hair exuded an air of an extremely young rock star or petty criminal. Teenagers all resemble young versions of older successes and failures. The possibilities are endless and all you want to do is find out which you are: when you're that young, success and failure are still binary.

With a slow blink, Kayla shifted her bag so that Catherine could sit.

'Did you stay here all night?' asked Catherine.

'No. I walked for most of it.'

'Are you all right?'

'Not really.'

Catherine flexed her foot. 'Good.'

Kayla turned, the sharpest move Catherine had seen her make. 'Why good?'

'Because people who walk all night and then sit on a park bench wearing a jacket on a hot day are either in a bad way and should be helped or batshit mad and must be avoided.' Kayla giggled and Catherine continued. 'If you'd said you were good, I'd have assumed that you were about to talk about aliens or Jesus and I would have to feign a seizure.'

Kayla murmured, tired but not sad, 'Just one of those bad nights.'

Catherine coddled Kayla's subsequent silence. She wondered what she could possibly offer this young woman, aside from fashion advice. Kayla began again.

'My Dad got taken away last night.'

'Oh, I'm sorry.'

'Have you had much to do with cops?'

'A little.'

'He's had a lot to do with them. I've only lived with him since he came out four years ago.'

'Prison?'

'Ten years for aggravated burglary and robbery.'

'Right.'

'This time they say it's murder.'

People were starting to walk around the street. A man in Ugg boots and a terry towelling hat was passing as she said the word "murder" and instinctively changed his trajectory further away from their seat.

'That's really hard.'

'He didn't do it.' She said it quickly, like a reflex.

'Does he have a lawyer?'

'He will. He called me instead of them though. He told me he had to go away again.' She shook her head. 'He shouldn't have called me.'

'Should he have called the lawyer?'

The girl crumbled in front of her, leaning forward on the bench, quietly sobbing. Catherine gently held her shuddering shoulders.

You can do very little for someone in crisis aside from listening and letting them know they are not alone: and one other thing.

'Do you want some food?'

'No, I should get home. I'm so tired I'm blubbing at strangers.' She smiled weakly. For a teenager who had been up all night, she was surprisingly polite and self-aware. Catherine warmed to her.

'I'm staying on the Avenue. Across from the football oval. If I can do anything, let me know. I have a friend who's a cop. Maybe she could answer some questions?'

Kayla stood up. 'Thanks, Catherine. If it was only the Dad thing, I would do that.'

'What else is it?'

Kayla rubbed at red eyes, wiping away the last of the tears. 'I think I've got personal enough this morning, don't you?' She forced a smile, and Catherine had the feeling that the teenager was talking more sense than she was. 'See you around.'

With that, she was gone, and suddenly Catherine was ready to go back to bed. The coffee shop, a winning option thirteen minutes ago, now seemed ridiculous; the sort of thing people did when they were at work.

She bought croissants at the supermarket; something she could eat after more sleep. Sleep was the key, then the beach, because she was most certainly not at work.

She told herself that all the way home.

Or would have, but she spent most of her working days walking and thinking about murder and hats, so damned if she was going to do it on holiday. To avoid the monotony of thinking of work, she had the choice of either skipping or walking along the beach.

She skipped towards it, wondering how long it would seem a good idea and if she had a hangover coming to greet her at 10am.

After six skips, the benefit of whimsy was outweighed by its effort, so she simply walked, thinking, despite herself, of murder and stab wounds.

You can ruin a holiday by trying too hard.

Catherine had noticed that the more people in the group, the more often this holiday pitfall happened, so as she was alone, there was no excuse. She just kept walking and thinking about murder, but in a holiday kind of way, as if she were putting tinsel on a computer screen in her metaphorical office.

To be thinking this way meant she was incredibly tired.

She passed a house that made her realise how gentrified the previous two blocks had been. The parched white weatherboard affair was ramshackle and almost beautiful with its mutt dog garden and hoarded junk spilling over the yard. The two cars in the front yard didn't look operational, though the tinny boat on a trailer, in what would have been traditionally called the driveway, looked well kept. It was the tinny that Catherine noticed, due to the sound.

The low buzzing was like a polite giant slowly shifting a rock around a corner so as not to make a fuss. Or perhaps the plug hole of the earth had finally been displaced and this was the first audible evidence of the coming draining of all society. Catherine moved cautiously towards it, unable to resist this alien sound. A slight fuzz and a subtle suck. A glacier-paced roll of thunder.

As she approached the tinny, she saw moisture underneath the stern. The boat had been used in the past few hours. The sound was still going, though the rational part of her mind was thinking CB radio or possum or...

The man's head came up so fast that for a microsecond Catherine thought he was some kind of boat centaur. The man, who Catherine would later realise had simply been snoring, moved from supine to upright in a time surely possible only for a gymnast.

The fellow was no gymnast. He was rotund, bedraggled and shaggy. He was also somewhere between forty and seventy, depending on his luck. He also seemed unhappy.

'No yabbies here,' he exclaimed. He was wearing a brown woollen jumper of a thickness normally only seen in the middle of winter.

'Of course not, sorry.' Catherine backed up, almost dropping the packet of croissants she held in her left hand.

A vein in his neck bulged. 'You don't need to be here. You can't be here.' The man was getting agitated. He squinted at her, and she instinctively knew he was about to feel around the boat, while continuing his squint. When he'd found his glasses, she had taken three steps back.

'Girl on a beach.'

'I'm sorry. I didn't mean to wake you. I–' She hesitated. 'I had never heard a sound like you snoring and got curious. Sorry.'

He tapped his left ear twice; he spoke, voice low. 'You saw small man's body. That made you in control. I saw that.'

Catherine didn't say anything. There wasn't much she could add.

The man suddenly looked away, over the side of the boat he was sitting in. He exhaled heavily, and Catherine looked down to see two large red eskies on the ground beside the boat. He turned back, almost sheepish. 'No harm here yet. You're not a bad one. Good you woke me. Arseholes can come early sometimes.' He nodded, agreeing with himself, and his extremely curly hair bounced in time.

He seemed more threatened than threat. Catherine was surprised by the lack of a dog that usually accompanied such displaced men.

Catherine smiled. 'Yep. No harm. I'm going now.'

'Yep. Good one. Go now.' He wasn't smiling anymore.

Catherine felt a high of adrenaline that she knew would recede in about four minutes. Just the time it took her to go home.

3

*If you smile like you know their secrets and you shake their hand just right, they'll
think you're what they've been waiting for.*

~ Brandon Miles-Barclay

Moments of extreme pleasure and pain cannot be remembered, for the sake of human psychology, but we have an inkling that one of the most delicious moments in life comes in the form of going back to bed in the morning.

Night sleeping is a necessity, a chore at times. Catherine struggled not to resent it. But morning sleep was a gift taken from the lap of the Gods, ignoring the glory of the sun and all the washing up that goes with it.

Catherine sometimes referred to it as "melty cheese sleep", when bones, skin and worries dissolved into a consistent ooze that was all the best and most peaceful stuff of living and death combined.

At any rate, the day was well into double digits before she awoke the second time, to the smell of the croissants that Britt had decided she would wait for no longer.

Britt obviously heard her coming, because a mug of coffee was presented to her as she entered the open plan kitchen.

Catherine bowed low. 'You are a Goddess.'

Britt's other hand was covered by an oven mitt in the shape of a kangaroo; her hair was up in a high ponytail, which made her eyebrows severe. 'It's been said by many. I don't know why they haven't made a statue yet.'

'The problem is your commitment to the homicide squad. You hide the Goddess within for the copper exterior. The crims would enjoy being interviewed by someone famous.'

'So many egos, so few jail cells.'

A croissant on a plate landed in front of Catherine; Britt had rustled up ham and cheese and Catherine pictured a statue out on the Ocean Grove main street, Britt holding a pastry to the sky. Catherine would at the very least attempt a sandcastle of it later in the day.

'Not that there's any egos in Homicide.'

Britt sat, pastry in one hand, paper in the other. 'No, none. We're practically Buddhist monks.'

'There are probably some egos in Tibet too.'

'Yeah, but they try to suppress them.' There was a beat as Catherine chewed and smelled the coffee. She could feel the air changing and wanted to enjoy a perfect moment.

Britt spoke. 'I've been thinking about yesterday.'

'The swim last night?' Catherine said dully.

Britt smiled wanly. 'No.'

'Oh, the case then.'

Britt scrunched her nose. 'It's not a case. I'm on holiday. Just the body and photos and the…' She trailed off, her hand doing a version of Queen Elizabeth's best wave, talking it through.

'You want to know more.' Catherine pushed the plate away and felt the heat of the mug against her palm.

'I don't think it's a poor use of our time. A man has died. I'm a detective, you're a…' she paused.

'Milliner.'

'Who's smarter than I am.'

Catherine's gut twisted at how much she enjoyed that. 'Don't flatter.'

'I think we could–' Britt's hand did some more work, '–spend a bit of time on it.'

Catherine took a long sip of coffee to disguise how she felt. 'Britt. You work. You sleep, some nights. People are going to die 365 days a year and for 330 days a year, that's your problem. Don't you need a break?'

'I swam in the ocean drunk last night and guess what, no one even stole my wallet. If I brought that up at work, they would be disappointed. I am trying, Catherine, but there's something about this. I just think…'

'You don't even know who's on the investigation.'

'No idea.'

'If you did know, you wouldn't go there.'

Britt walked over to the sink with Catherine's plate. 'Of course not. It would be disrespectful.'

'But you don't know, so it's your case.'

'I thought about it all night. It feels like my case.'

Catherine stood up and stretched theatrically.

'Why are you doing that?' Britt asked, leaning against the fridge.

Catherine looked up from almost touching her toes. 'Oh, what? I was just thinking you should find out who's on the case, you know. Break the rules a little and make a call. Then I'm going to thrash you at beach volleyball.'

Britt snorted. 'Catherine, I train every day and you think walking to the Glasgow Palace for a gin is exercise.'

Catherine flexed her neck in a way that made a lovely cracking sound. 'Sorry?' She flexed her shoulders. 'I heard fear in your voice, but didn't hear the words.'

Britt walked down the stairs, towards the shed where the sports equipment was kept. 'You're going down, Kint. I will bury you.'

Catherine smiled and kept stretching.

It was a matter of seconds before Boris started to choke. As he kept his feet moving, the air came hot and thick through his mouth. Catherine had told him to count his steps. After two, he lost count and felt the futility of his life. He saw a gap in the traffic and pushed, finding some life in his legs as he avoided the semi-trailer bearing down on him. There was noise all around him. Sirens, engines, and wheels. With one last burst, he pushed onwards and upwards towards higher ground. A voice called out in defeat and only he recognised it as his own.

He had missed the train by seconds.

Catherine's advice, as it regularly was in both the business and pleasure aspects of their friendship, had not helped the situation. He gave a small smile at the thought of telling her about it later.

Panting, he wiped sweat from his brow and wished he'd remembered deodorant. He threw down his canvas bag, sat in the sunshine and stared at the tracks of the Upfield Line as they hummed in the heat of midday.

As he rubbed his eyes, he wondered why he felt light. Then it hit him.

He was feeling light because for three minutes, as he ran for the train, he hadn't been thinking about Molly.

And now she was back, as she had been for the past month. Dancing in front of him with a face that shifted from coquettish to a scowl. Somewhere between taking him back and never speaking to him again.

Knowing it was coming, Boris closed his eyes futilely against the next image. Molly with someone else. Boris could never see details of the other men. Just that they were smart and thin and had enough money. Sometimes he heard her whispering about plane flights and holidays.

And the copulating. These mystery men were stallions. The reels of endless passion that he imagined her in had made him feel dehydrated.

'The next train from platform one will be the twelve thirty-four to Flinders Street, stopping all stations to Flinders Street, via the City Loop.'

The announcement stopped Molly in a particularly defiant flourish that would test any human hamstring. Boris saw the train coming, glimmering in the heat and light. As he stepped on, he felt the conditioned air envelop him and was suddenly aware of how much he was sweating. Thankfully, the carriage was mostly empty, and he could sit alone without worrying about his armpits ruining anyone else's trip. He rested his head against the glass and watched the graffiti and corrugated iron mix with the boutique fencing of some of the prettier houses. He fondled his phone in his pocket. Thought about taking it out, looking at the photos. The same photos he'd been looking at endlessly for the past twenty-seven days.

'I think it's done.'

'What?'

'Us.' She smiled a little.

'Is this because I ordered the Parma?'

'No, Boris. It's just that the past two weeks have been hard, and if there are two hard weeks after only four months. I think it's done.'

They ate. Boris paid. She left. He had ordered a pint and sat for a full twenty minutes before he called Catherine.

And now today. Day twenty-eight. As the train passed through the rail yards of North Melbourne, he again agreed with Molly's logic. Some couples don't fight at all; yet they fought. And it was early days.

Boris looked at his hands and spread his fingers. Come on, see some positives. He had a week off from work at the Glasgow Palace: no pub, no kegs, and no manager. He was going to the beach with his friends. With Catherine on holiday too, the chances of needing to step up as her muscle in any wild goose chase was also minimal. All he had to do was not be a grumpy sad twit and all would be well. Life has its ups and downs. See, here's a tunnel, this is a dark bit of the journey, see what happens now? It lights up, it's okay again.

He looked at his reflection in the window. Fantastic, Boris. Compare your life to the Upfield train line. Everything will be ok, mate, because eventually you get to bloody Flagstaff. Even Pollyanna would roll her eyes at that one.

His mood hadn't lifted by the end of the loop tunnels and Flinders Street. The next stop would be Southern Cross. Where he would meet Andy, and hit the rails for Geelong. 'Lord God,' he muttered. 'May Andy have a few traveller beers in his bag and something other than his new girlfriend to talk about.' The train bumped, as if it had heard his prayers.

Just 375 seconds later, and on a different train, Andy was talking. 'My God. Seriously. She has this laugh. It's like the most amazing music I've ever heard.'

Boris' head collided with train glass for the second time that day. Andy didn't even pause for breath.

'I just never thought it would happen. You know? I mean, you always hear it, don't you? Thunderbolts? The sky is on fire, the oxygen is perfect. I guessed that either everyone was having me on. Or.' He paused.

Boris rubbed his face against the glass. 'Or it will happen to everyone but you.'

Andy grinned. 'Yeah. Exactly, man.'

Boris ran a hand through his hair. Looked back at Andy, who was smiling awkwardly, as if he had spilled a drink.

'Shite. Ah, Boris.'

Every time Andy said his name, his Scots accent became more pronounced. If Andy said railway, rodent or rumpus, his r was soft, with Boris, for some reason, you got the full hard roll.

'Yeah, mate?'

'I'm sorry. I'm going on and on about Bernadette and, well, you must be thinking about someone too.'

Boris looked away through the window. Werribee was going past at an unhurried rate. 'Don't say that.'

'What?'

'If you're talking about Bernadette and I'm struggling, and you don't notice because you're all loved up, that's fine. If you notice I'm struggling, and apologise, then I'm bringing you down.'

'You couldn't bring me down this week, pal.'

'Okay. Well, we should celebrate that. I'm sick of being grumpy.'

'Want me to tell you about the nights?'

Boris groaned.

'I'm joking, man.'

Boris had never seen the Scotsman so completely happy. In fact, after months of watching Andy's Quixotic and unsuccessful quest to win Catherine's heart, this was an improvement.

'Okay. When do we get to meet her?'

Andy smiled at the roof of the train. 'She's quite busy. She's one of the top Public Servants in Premier and Cabinet.' His voice slowed as he tried to recall a title. 'Deputy Communications and Systems something – I think.' He leaned in. 'It's a honeymoon period, of course, but she's even talking about me leaving the Zoo and just taking care of her. How about that? No more admin?'

'Just cooking for her and the Premier.'

'I'm man enough for that.' Andy's chest puffed. 'It's the 21st century. I can be a kept man.'

Boris held his hands up. 'I didn't mean that, mate. Shit, I remember having similar conversations with Molly. She wanted me out of the pub.' He grinned slowly. 'Maybe we're the kind that needs saving.'

Andy raised an eyebrow. 'Oh yeah. You're a delicate flower.'

They paused awhile. In the distance, Boris looked for the You Yangs. The mountain range provided the only thing to look at between Melbourne and Geelong.

Andy's voice was high and quiet. 'She did ask me.'

'What, marriage?'

Andy shook his head, 'No. I mean, she did mention that, but. In the first week, she asked me–'

Boris leaned in. 'What?'

'She asked me to buy her tampons.'

Boris waited for the punchline. 'And?'

'Don't you think that's weird?'

'No.'

'Really?'

Boris thought a second. 'No.'

'Sorry.' Andy swallowed. 'It's just. I've never been asked before. I found it a bit…icky.'

Boris smiled. 'A lot of human stuff is icky mate. Even the best bits.'

'Yeah, I get that, but, I mean, did you buy them for Molly?'

'Sometimes, it's pretty easy once you know the right brand. But, my best friend is a woman. We do things for each other. Catherine's bought me underpants when I was in need. I'm sure she'd find that ickier. She's not even a lover.'

'Right. Glad I didn't make a thing of it with Bernie then.'

'Played it cool?'

'As a cucumber.'

'Good man.' Boris rubbed his chin. 'Maybe I thought it was odd when I first bought a pack, but no one cares. Periods happen one week out of four, so I guess that means a quarter of women around us are going through it at any given time.'

'Right.' Andy nodded. 'The least we can do is help with the shopping.'

'Totally.'

The mountains and plains started giving way to the suburbia of Geelong.

Catherine watched the ball bounce in her court and felt the need to mention a dense book she had just finished. As Britt quietly whooped, Catherine concluded that volleyball was a frivolous waste of time, which for her – who usually adored frivolous wastes of time – took some doing. Britt did a cartwheel as Catherine fetched the ball and prepared to serve.

'I'm only letting you win to improve your mood, you know.' She pushed the ball high over the net, trying to put Britt's eye line in the sun.

Britt volleyed easily. 'You have never let anyone win in your life.'

'Oh please. I'm a paragon of generosity. Boris has won two–' she somehow got a hand to the ball at knee height. '–games of gin now.'

Britt backed up and dug the ball high. 'Out of four hundred games.'

Catherine rose to spike. 'You make it sound like Thomas' case clearance.'

Britt sprawled and missed. She glared daggers at Catherine from her momentary sandy resting place. 'That will only work once.'

'What?' Catherine was aware of her strut. Butter wouldn't melt in her mouth.

'Detective Luke arsing Thomas. Here.' Britt's hands spread towards the cloudless sky. 'I spend every week at work near the dickhead and now he's here too.'

'You're the one who called to find out who was on the case. Plus, you don't have to work with him this week.'

'No, but I'll possibly see him find the most vulnerable person close by and beat a confession out of them. He's a prick, he profiles, he's classist and sexist.' She beat the ball high over Catherine's head. Swore at the mis-serve.

Catherine called over her shoulder, 'You never mentioned sexist before.'

'Yes, I did. He's the one that made the joke at the Christmas party.'

Catherine's eyes widened. 'Oh Christ, that guy.'

'You're with me now?'

Catherine served low; Britt lobbed high. Catherine leapt to spike. 'So, let's suit up.' She mishit, and the ball spilled left.

Britt retrieved the ball and checked her watch. 'We have to get Boris and Andy soon. Shall we both go?'

'I fancy a few minutes' contemplation. How about you go?'

'I fancy a swim. How about you go?'

Catherine turned; the water was glistening. No one ever regretted a swim, aside from a certain Prime Minister. Perhaps contemplation could be taken from the surf. 'It's all on the last point. Loser plays taxi.'

Britt rolled her neck. 'Done.'

Catherine paused, bouncing the ball, ostensibly to maintain conversation, but Britt would have noticed her breathing was getting heavy. 'I mean it about suiting up. If Thomas is as bad as you say, we should spend some time on this. Boris will be grateful for the distraction.'

'I'm not sure I can risk my ankle at this stage.'

Catherine snorted. 'That was hardly his fault, and you weren't directly working with him then. I've done lots with him, mostly without injury.'

'Sure; to you.'

Catherine pushed it high and drifting to the left, Britt pushed it back and Catherine had to scramble a dig over her shoulder to return. Britt sidestepped, then adjusted as she corrected her trajectory backwards, getting to the ball easily but not moving it where she wanted.

Catherine moved right and pushed it over, only to see the ball return hard to the left. The wind had come up and she noticed the ripple of the net. The thought of a drive to Geelong filled her vision and she worked her legs, reaching the ball with a second to spare. As the ball eased over the net towards Britt, Catherine gave a turn and called out 'Duc!' in a delighted voice.

Britt's volley sailed into the net and she turned her head in anticipation of an approaching policeman only to see a dark haired boy of seven walking a small scotch terrier.

Britt gave a guttural howl. 'Kint! That was low.'

Catherine scratched her head as her breathing came back to normal. 'Oh gosh. I was sure that was Duc.'

'You're a witch and a con artist.'

'And you're a taxi. Maybe I should get my eyes checked.'

Britt gave another groan. Catherine waved at the boy, who waved back and grinned. He had a bottom tooth missing.

Catherine was sure Duc would have approved. She could imagine him laughing as she walked towards the surf.

By the time Britt had got back and showered, she was going to be twenty-five minutes early for the train. She could have had that swim after all. Sabotaged, once again, by her own efficiency.

She considered the kettle, decided she was caffeinated enough, and picked up the local paper again. Greens candidate Brandon Miles-Barclay stared out from the front page. Handsome, his dark hair tousled by the wind while he stood in a grey suit on what must have been a cooler month down at Thirteenth Beach. Britt read the story. Few details yet, though it was mentioned that he was not, as previously reported, last seen on a boat.

With Thomas investigating, Britt knew corners would be cut. The big man arrested last night would fit the bill. He ticked the boxes of working class, violent and, according to Catherine, with previous criminal form. Thomas kept the numbers up in homicide, but Britt knew the emperor had no clothes. He was a bully and a hustler. She suspected her boss, Williams, thought the same, but she had given up guessing what Williams really thought long ago.

Except she knew what he would think of her interfering with an investigation.

She went down the stairs and got into her Green Mitsubishi. The radio came alive with the news as soon as she turned the key. Political scandal, sports triumph, then a murder. Her job was usually the third story of almost every bulletin. Being on holiday meant that right now it wasn't her job. She said it out loud, twice.

Her phone call to the office had told her Selena Perfetto, the new woman in homicide, was with Thomas. She might keep him diligent.

Slowly and deliberately, Britt changed the station. Music. Holiday. She could even dance in the car.

To the strain of a weeping guitar, she drove past the main drag towards Geelong. A familiar figure made her swear under her breath. The traffic was slow, so she couldn't miss Thomas on the path. All coiffed hair and cream suit. The man had a swagger even when he wasn't walking. Perfetto looked on as Thomas talked to the rat-faced man who had been with the man arrested last night. Britt pulled over to watch.

Both men were short. Perfetto was the tallest of the trio even in flats. Thomas was counting on his fingers.

Britt had heard this spiel: he was given his "options" talk, made up of coming quietly for a chat, going loudly for a formal interview, or a silence that stretched for years in a big building with poor food. He always sounded more like a car salesman than a cop when he did it. Ratface was listening impassively. It's hard to be impassive to a homicide cop unless you've done it before. Britt guessed this fellow was some kind of player.

When Thomas was done, Ratface brought up his own fingers and gave three options of his own. These culminated in a middle finger being extended into Thomas' face, before Ratty walked off.

Thomas started after him, with Perfetto putting a firm hand out. Even from fifty metres away Britt could see Thomas redden, but he stopped, nodded.

Perfetto walked away. Only two months into the job, she was the only other woman in homicide. Britt had avoided her, loathe to become "the girls" in the team. Maybe she had made a mistake. Perfetto, she decided, was all right.

Catherine was momentarily blinded by the sun as she came in from the surf. Between the reflection on the shallows and the actual sun, the world became a sheer white glow, which gave her the impression of being reborn as a spark in the centre of the universe. That changed quickly as she became overwhelmed with the smell of cheap bourbon and coke.

A figure loomed in front of her, swaying slightly. A large man, but short. The sun was behind him, so Catherine couldn't make out his features, but the wild curls escaping from his truckers cap identified him as the man who slept in a dinghy. Catherine changed her trajectory to circumnavigate the fellow, who was stumbling to follow her.

'You're a lucky one.' His voice was gentle, compared with this morning. It seemed absent of sleaze, which was a relief, but it could still be coming.

'Yes, lovely day,' she replied neutrally.

'You have lots of lucky days. I can tell.'

He had stopped moving, which gave Catherine the choice of following her instinct for safety and walking away, or yielding to her instinct for intrigue and giving him a minute. She stayed put.

'How do you see luck?'

He laughed a singsong kind of laugh. 'When you have none, you see it in some others. Sometimes they can wash off on you. You're not just here for swimming, are you?'

Again, Catherine could detect no threat or sleaze, despite the strange words. 'What do you mean?'

'You were looking for someone this morning. You're looking for answers. Old Golledge can tell.'

Catherine's shoulders slumped. 'If you so much as whisper the word Jesus, I'll kick you.'

The man shook his head. 'I've never met him.'

'Glad to hear.'

'I wouldn't mind, sometimes.'

Catherine walked towards her towel. The sand was warm under her feet. She focused on it and sought patience from it. He tottered behind her at a respectful distance.

'There's things happening here.'

'Always things happening. It's a busy planet. For example, I have a busy day.'

'Me too. I just wanted to tell you I don't like cops.'

Catherine voice was low. 'Why would I care about that?'

The man sat down. Catherine was unsure if he had a choice in the matter or the bourbon was taking effect. 'Some people do things that cops don't like, but they don't hurt people. I just don't want to be confused with someone who hurts people. I'm just Golledge, you know?

Catherine picked up the volleyball and arranged the towel around her shoulders. 'Right now, you're just boring one person.'

'Don't creep up on sleeping people.' As he said this, a cloud drifted over the sun, adding to the melodrama.

Catherine suppressed an eyeroll. 'I'll avoid you in any state.'

He wasn't getting the hint, which Catherine should have seen coming. 'I don't hurt people.'

'Then why am I getting a headache?'

'You're lucky. I know a good man with herbs.' He looked sleepy but laughed a little to himself.

'I'm not sure you know what luck is.' She started toward the stairs, away from the beach.

'It's a wind that sits on your shoulder and no one else sees it,' he called to her as she walked away.

She didn't look back until she was at the top of the stairs. He was gone. Not only from the spot he'd been in, but completely, even though Catherine could see vast amounts of the beach. She wouldn't have thought a world class sprinter could have cleared so much space so quickly, let alone a large man with a gutful of booze.

'A bourbon and coke shaman. That's what the planet needs.'

She was about to walk home when she saw thirty people holding hands in the dunes.

Britt turned down the radio as she pulled in beside the train station. Catherine would have laughed at her listening unironically to the Classic Hits station, though Boris would probably sing along. The train had just come to a stop. Even on holiday, she was on time. Which, she noted, wouldn't happen at work, when she'd be seven minutes early.

Work. Everyone's still at it, she thought, watching men and women in hi-vis conducting slow roadworks in the heat. She rubbed her eyes. Only seven more days and she'd be back at work and nothing else would have to make sense. She found the thought comforting and knew she shouldn't. You couldn't be a cop all the time, or you'd end up like–

She didn't even want to finish the thought.

Among the throng, she picked out Boris and Andy: Boris in an orange tee shirt with a small backpack and Andy looking suspiciously ironed for a man on a holiday and walking in front of a suitcase on wheels.

'Hi, Britt.' Boris kissed her cheek. 'Thanks, we could have got the bus.'

'No Catherine?' Andy asked. Britt wasn't sure, but for a second his voice broke a little.

'She wanted to think.'

Andy looked at his watch. 'Oh, I suppose it is after three, almost. She's at the pub?' He got his suitcase into the boot on the second try.

'No, mate. *Think*.' Boris smiled and Britt wondered how much he was guessing.

'What's she got to think about, she's on holiday?' Andy got into the back seat, more focused on his seatbelt than the conversation. 'If she's not at the pub, could we get her there?'

Boris cracked his neck. 'She's not thinking about a body that came up on the beach yesterday, is she?'

Britt smiled quietly. He was the least cop kind of man she knew, but every now and again, Britt thought that was a shame.

'Oh, God, not again,' came a voice from the back seat as the engine started.

4

Humans have survived by running away for more than 200 million years.
Why on earth do cowards still have a bad name?

~ Andy McCafferty

A circle of roughly forty people were on the beach, augmented by at least five dogs. Some of them were holding hands and some were leaning on each other. They stretched almost to the dunes, at the highest point of the beach. They gathered loosely around a woman with fierce eyes and a plait hanging over her right shoulder.

Catherine approached slowly. No one seemed to notice her coming. As she stepped towards them, she began to hear the woman's words as she addressed the throng. The first words were of loyalty and praise. Catherine wondered if she was sneaking up on a cult, but then the purpose became clear.

'He is lost, and that is horrible. His cause, however, is not. It cannot be lost and will not be lost. The move to have a more progressive world is bigger than one man, even one as great as Brandon.' She paused, obviously composing herself. She breathed in and out three times. Her voice was unsteady but she pushed through. 'We will work in his memory and stand on the shoulders of his achievements. We will push forward proudly in the values that he championed. We will win the support of those who had not ever seen us previously as anything but outsiders. This was a political death.' She paused. 'But we will strive to celebrate and continue the memory of his political life. We will not be cowed.'

There were strong calls of support, though Catherine caught at least one person rolling their eyes. The woman went on, unaware of any disdain. 'After the election, we can mourn. Today, we need to be strong and remember the great man Brandon was, what he stood for and how he was never afraid to take a stand. Today, we walk in the imprint of his footsteps and continue our revolution.'

Great applause greeted this. Catherine was moved, even if it was because the speech was short.

A couple with guitars took the woman's place. Catherine steeled herself for terrible Bob Marley, and then, when they started a song of their own composition, Catherine wished they were playing Bob Marley. Instinctively, possibly because she hated earnestness from any political side, she sought out one of the eye rollers.

Aside from tips of neon blue, her wavy hair was completely black. The tips bounced between her shoulders and her dark face. She gave Catherine a nod and a smile that seemed undeserved.

'That was lovely, don't you think?' The woman's voice was even, but Catherine immediately thought of one of the few Vietnamese words she knew, aside from the number system: *sao-qua*, a playful version of "you're a liar". She decided she had little to lose and waited until she and this woman were out of earshot.

'Yes, aside from the fact that I think she's full of shit.'

The woman's eyes glowed briefly, dulling to neutral as if by reflex. Her mouth twitched as she held her hand out. 'I don't think I know you.'

'You don't, but don't worry. I don't know you either. I'm Catherine.'

'Yvonne McSweeney.' Her handshake was firm but not overpowering. Catherine was on a roll, so she tried again.

'Good handshake, first and surname, you smile instinctively when you don't know someone. You're a politician.'

Yvonne exhaled a half laugh out of her nose, then rubbed her chin. 'Attentive, nosey, smart, but needs people to know it. You're not a cop, I would say journo, but that doesn't fit. Are you something else, but wish you were a cop?'

Catherine made a sound like a tired horse entering a lake. She had a sudden need to look at the musicians, who were doing to harmony what worms do to apples. She bit her lip. 'Milliner. Ex-crime scene investigation. I did eighteen days of Police academy.'

They had made their way to the edge of the group. From somewhere unknown, a slab of beer had appeared, and both now had a drink in hand. Yvonne cracked open her can.

'Eighteen days is a fine amount of time to try something. I played the damn clarinet for almost a decade.'

'Are you elected?'

'Not yet.'

Catherine did a slow blink. 'Did I miss your speech?'

'You must have,' she said breezily. 'Currently I'm working in the campaign office. Are you even a Greens member?'

Catherine shook her head. 'Even when the cause is just, I'm not a joiner. Police Academy taught me that. Are you down from Melbourne?'

'No. I'm local.'

Catherine nodded at the speaker, who was talking earnestly among a group of green tee-shirted mourners. 'Who's she?'

'She.' Yvonne took a contemplative sip. 'Is Shelby Acland. Her Dad was one of the founding members of the Geelong branch. I suspect that in the coming days she'll be announced as Brandon's replacement.'

'I see. What're her policies?'

'I don't know. I didn't hear much about them then: nothing about Torquay, nothing about marine protection, nothing about multiculturalism. Just a lot of stuff about The Cause, without saying what that is. That's what gets you the nod.'

'Instead of you?'

Yvonne's eyes widened. 'I try not to be too transparent. Is it working that badly?'

'Everyone in politics wants to be Prime Minister, right? Isn't it better when everyone acknowledges that?'

'Hmm.' Yvonne shook her head. 'No. It's better when you have a world of happy background Mercutios and a Romeo out front to answer to all of them.'

Catherine giggled. 'So that's why Macbeth was a better play.'

'At least more realistic. Nice meeting you.' Yvonne moved on as two women in suits came towards her. She was shaking their hands warmly as Catherine finished her drink and silently cancelled her non-existent Greens membership. She found her way back to the stairs, took a final look for the strange Mr Golledge, then, finding nothing, returned home.

Boris blinked, horrified, at their triumphant faces. Oh God, he had zoned out again.

Catherine's voice rang out, 'And yes, that is forty-five seconds.'

Boris groaned. Around him, Britt, Andy and Catherine barely suppressed laughter. Andy held out an empty plastic jug and patted him consolingly on the shoulder.

Boris took it resignedly. 'I swear it didn't seem that long.' He rubbed his beard.

'It never does, but if we're not on top of this, you're going to spend the entire time here sulking.' Catherine's eyes were brighter than usual, even in the extreme lighting of the Zebra bar. 'This penance is the best thing for you.'

Boris rose. 'I didn't realise you had stopped talking.'

'For the last thirty seconds I've had my hands over my ears, Catherine her eyes and Andy his mouth.' Britt pointed. 'That waitress thought we were trolling you.'

'Well, weren't you?'

Catherine rose with him. 'Nonsense. We're all here to talk, to laugh and to commiserate. All you have to do is stop vagueing off. Be in the moment.'

'I was in the moment.'

'It was a sulky moment.'

He shrugged. While the bar was busy, the line for drinks was relatively short and so a few minutes later Boris was accepting – and paying for, penance is penance – a jug of lager and a gin and tonic for Catherine.

Boris tried to keep from sounding churlish. 'I've never been good at the "just snap out of it" thing. Mourning is part of the human condition.'

Catherine nodded wisely. 'Yes, yes, except when you're mourning an idea rather than a human and it's not someone dying but a girl who was probably going to annoy you eventually, deciding that you were annoying her first. If I truly thought she was your soulmate, I would be weeping with you. But no. She isn't and I'm not. Plenty more fish in the sea.'

Boris poured Andy and Britt their beer before emptying the jug into his own pint glass. 'Oh, Christ. Don't start that. There should be a "check your privilege" thing for pretty people.'

Britt nodded, agreeing. 'Yes, Catherine, we don't know how lucky we are.'

'No, we really don't,' chimed in Andy. 'The fact that you're practically a superhero just never comes up.'

Boris grinned, despite himself. 'I'm not and it doesn't.'

Andy clapped him on the back. 'You've done more heroic things than most on the planet and yet any time there's romance involved you haven't quite got past Teenage Angst 101.' He gestured with his hand as if trying to wield a spell. 'You have to remember who you are and what you can do. The lives you've saved.'

Catherine joined in. 'The skylights you've cracked.'

Britt snorted. 'The ankles you've broken.' Andy almost spat beer at that.

Boris gestured understanding with his beer. 'Thanks. I get all that and I appreciate where it comes from. I will try. Again, Britt, I'm sorry about your ankle.'

She echoed his toast. 'Points for running towards a gunman.'

'So, if I vague off now I'm thinking about my future love, not my past. Kindly stop the game.'

Catherine made a noise like a quiz show buzzer. 'No, you're a serial offender. You must learn to embrace the challenges of romance. Warts and all.'

She looked up as Britt stood, her eyes towards the bar. 'What?'

Britt moved past her quickly. 'I'm embracing the challenge myself.'

Catherine waited a moment before she turned. Boris was already watching as Britt sidled next to Constable Duc Nguyen, looking better in civvies than he did in his uniform, as far as Catherine was concerned.

Boris burped quietly. 'Who's that?'

'Local cop. He was with us when we found the body.'

'Very prominent cheekbones. Definitely your type.'

Catherine inhaled deeply and sipped gin. 'Yep, knew I shouldn't have taken the window seat.'

Boris patted her shoulder. 'You can be quiet for a while. I won't play.'

'Double huh.' Catherine twirled ice in her glass and tried to enjoy oxygen and not look at the bar again. The music in the air was almost passable and she had Boris and Andy to talk to.

Her drink empty, this suddenly seemed a trifecta of disappointment. Catherine closed her eyes and reflected on the following reality: Having tall, ex-model cops as friends was occasionally going to complicate meeting attractive men.

The emptiness in the glass did, however, give her a *bona fide* reason to go back to the bar. As she stood, she pointed at the half full jug and Boris nodded. Andy called out, 'Hey? Isn't he supposed to be buying?'

'I veto his punishment, this one time.' Catherine called.

At the bar, she was delighted to see Duc turn his head towards her and smile.

'Hello. It's my favourite milliner.'

'And my favourite officer,' she returned. 'Aside from the detective here,' she added quickly. Britt smiled.

'Duc was refusing to give me an update on the case.'

Catherine patted his back. 'Good man. Have a drink?'

Britt gestured towards the table. 'Would you care to join us?'

'Love one. It's so nice when a cop isn't a pariah.'

Britt passed her glass to Catherine. 'It must mean you're drinking with cops.'

Catherine smiled, as they moved off while she waited for the order. She watched Duc shake Boris' hand easily, Andy was more reticent.

It was an interminable four minutes until the drinks came, and Catherine amused herself with a look around the bar. Of the forty or so people in the place, only four, she suspected, were local. Everyone had that glazed, flushed bearing of a holiday-maker, with families in various forms of bliss or contempt, and friends sitting in the chatter or silence that comes with being away from home.

Drinks finally in hand and paid for, she headed back to the table. Andy was in full flight.

'I guess you just have an idea of where a policeman would drink, and this isn't it.'

Duc opened his hands. 'Because it's a brightly lit bar and the television up there is continually showing party music from thirty years ago?'

'Yeah.' Andy gestured at the surroundings. 'Everyone is so... happy. Doesn't that bother you?'

Duc took a long sip, possibly aware that the Scotsman had had a good deal more refreshment than him. 'Well, I guess I could find a dingy pub with a tab where there are four other cops and we don't speak much aside from carrying the burden of the world on our shoulders.'

Britt looked down to avoid laughing. Andy didn't notice. 'Yeah?'

'But it's Geelong, and I live here, so I endure the happiness.' Duc smiled. 'Sometimes I even enjoy it.'

Boris nudged the Scotsman. 'Andy, pool table's free.'

Andy stood. 'Excuse me.' He warmed up a shoulder. 'I have to give this oaf a schooling.'

Catherine and Britt gave their attention to Duc, and noticed each other doing it. Catherine spoke first. 'So, if you can't talk about the Miles-Barclay case, what else are you working on?'

'Just keeping the peace in the war of the caravans.'

'Doesn't that happen every year?'

'To an extent. This year's worse because there's Greens and Labor volunteers in about a quarter of them. They're getting a bit Sharks and Jets.'

'Throwing manifestos at each other?' Britt chimed in.

'It got pretty low-brow last night. Neither side was giving great speeches.'

'I'm sure the volume was good though.'

Duc saluted with his glass. 'Yeah, pitch perfect.'

Britt swirled her glass. 'We saw the arrest last night. You're good at the job. Why are you still a connie?'

'I guess I'm lazy. They wanted me to be a Sergeant for a while. Also.' He paused, then shrugged. 'I ask questions.'

Britt smiled. 'Not a favourite at the station?'

'Not everyone's, no. I've been pushing on a few things.'

'Like the murder?'

Duc shook his head, not biting.

'Okay you can't talk about that,' said Catherine. 'What else is happening in this seaside paradise?'

'Nothing as sexy. I'm sure its small beans compared to Melbourne.'

'In Melbourne I get to live in a different suburb to the people I'm chasing. This local stuff is hard.'

Duc smiled a little at that. 'That's a good point. I've been frustrated for a year about seahorse poaching. No one wants to touch it, but there's not many of them left.' His face creased as he spoke. Catherine noted that, by comparison, he seemed jovial when discussing the murder.

'Why don't people want to touch it?'

'Doesn't compare to crimes against people, plus you end up annoying your neighbours. There's also a cross-agency aspect as a lot of the horses are smuggled to Asia for eastern medicine. Most of the folk I talk to say it's an AFP thing.'

Britt grunted. 'The Feds? They're great at the airport; haven't been impressed anywhere else.'

Duc nodded. 'Anyway, I've made some people at work a bit uncomfortable.'

Catherine sipped her drink thoughtfully. 'What are they poached for?'

'Asthma. Insomnia. Impotence. Skin infections.' Duc had done his research. 'Mostly impotence.'

'Tell me more.'

Britt made a hard sound into her beer.

'Let's leave it. The brass has warned me to be more focused on burglaries and domestic violence.' He let out a sigh.

'It's a great job, but it'll take over everything else.' Britt shook her head ruefully. Duc didn't seem to register.

'Anyway, tell me about hats,' he grinned, and Catherine was only vaguely aware of Britt leaving the table to watch the pool game.

Two hours later, the four of them walked up a moonlit road away from town. Catherine was singing to the stars while she held onto Boris' neck. Andy and Britt were close by, deep in conversation about Bernadette.

'On the other side of the galaxyyyyyyy.'

In the darkness, no one could have seen Britt roll her eyes. 'I really don't understand how you got to the "singing at the stars" stage quicker than the rest of us.'

'Chips.' Catherine pointed with her finger. 'You had chips. I saw you.'

'We didn't want to interrupt your date.' Britt's voice was, any witness would agree, completely even.

'Not a date, detective. Just a bit of a chat. Shame he had an early shift tomorrow though.' Her wink used the whole of her body.

'A responsible officer.' Britt sniffed. 'Such judgment.'

Andy giggled. Britt hit him ungently.

Catherine pointed. 'I don't see how it's his fault.'

'Neither do I.' Andy rubbed his shoulder.

Boris grunted. 'I swear the walk *to* the pub wasn't this long.'

Catherine was about to agree and point out that he wasn't carrying her then. The words didn't come due to a screech of tyres as a car came around the corner at speed. The avenue they were walking down was bereft of streetlamps and so the headlights dominated their vision. The car slowed.

Boris and Catherine moved left, Catherine clinging to the burly man's back; Britt and Andy went to the right. The car rolled slowly down the street, its interior dark. About 20 metres away from them it stopped, without turning its motor off.

'If that was a dog, I'd throw it a stick.' Catherine grinned, Boris turned his head, but didn't get the joke either.

'I wish I had a stick.' Britt said quietly.

Andy seemed very interested in the side of the street as the other three stood on the road. The car didn't move, nor did its lights switch off. Boris could see the numberplate was dark with white lettering, but no detail was discernible.

Boris started to walk forward.

'Hang on, Boris.' Britt called.

'I can't ignore it.'

She put a hand on his shoulder. 'Let a cop do it.' She walked past him.

Boris had to admit, she walked with real poise, even after consuming a decent amount of lager. Boris walked slowly behind her, leaving a gap of twenty metres between him and Britt. Catherine walked with him, her breathing even.

Britt closed in on the car, her hand out in an antiquated 'stop thief' pose. Boris tensed, calculating how much time Britt would have to roll if the car accelerated. Then how much time he would have. He noticed Catherine was swaying slightly. He took that into account and scanned the surroundings. An agapanthus bush looked softer than most of the fences; he would roll there.

The car's engine spluttered, stalled, then started at the second attempt. Britt's knees bent, ready to run or jump, but the car went into reverse, away from her. It jolted backwards and to the left, almost backing into a picket fence before the car rolled forward and away from them, accelerating as fast as it had approached. Boris let out a breath.

Catherine swore quietly and long.

Suddenly, Andy was beside them. Boris had the feeling he'd been jogging to catch up. 'Did you get the number plate?'

In the gloom, Britt shook her head. 'I didn't. I could barely see anything on it. I think it was cream, but that's about it. Did you get it, Boris?'

'Nah, too dark.' He scratched his beard. 'Kids larking, you think?'

Andy giggled 'Larking? I swear your language is from the last world war.'

Boris stifled a groan. 'Well, what do you think?'

'I've only been here seven hours. I haven't offended anyone yet.' He swallowed. 'Matter of fact, it's only with you folk I even think like that.'

Britt looked back to the road the car had disappeared down. 'I haven't annoyed anyone either. It's been quite nice, really. Catherine?'

'Only you that I'm aware of, detective.'

They started walking again.

Britt snorted. 'Yes well, not your fault he's not into stunning blondes.'

Catherine put an arm around her. 'I think you're beautiful, Britt.'

Britt joined the embrace. 'Too soon, honey. Let's talk about hats.'

5

Some police work is watching closely and noticing when someone screws up.

~ Britt Houden

Boris was rubbing his eyes before he knew he was awake. For a confused second, he thought he was at home with Molly, then the memory came. No Molly, no more. The breathing he could hear was not his beautiful girlfriend, but the rhythmic wheeze of a Scots admin clerk. Boris rubbed his belly and sniffed. Reality can be incredibly draining.

Why am I awake? He thought in the darkness, then his abdomen answered, and he knew why he needed to get up.

3am bathroom breaks are the curse of all beer drinkers. Boris knew that if he ever had children, his body would already be used to interrupted sleep.

He padded down the hall, thought twice outside the door, unsure if it was the bathroom or a broom cupboard. He took a gamble and headed in. No brooms fell on his head and, a minute later, he no longer needed the bathroom.

He went back to the hallway and for a second felt a physical pain in his chest. He winced, even though he knew it wasn't a heart attack, nor indigestion. Just the absence of someone to go back to bed with, a loneliness that threatened to be the defining emotion of his life. He rested his head against the cool doorframe and wondered when the hell he had decided thoughts like that were acceptable, even late at night?

He considered whether to feel awful sitting up or lying down. He chose sitting up, because then at least he could pretend he would feel better lying down. He found a light switch and illuminated his way to the sunroom, wondering what the hell a sunroom is called at 3am. He slid the glass door closed and shut himself off from the rest of the house.

Before he turned on the room's small lamp, he saw the car outside.

Large, cream, beat up. With just enough fog on the side window to indicate that someone was inside.

Boris rubbed his eyes, trying to wake up sufficiently to see the number plate in the dimly lit street. On the table beside him was a crossword, half done. A scramble yielded a pen and he took down what he could make out of the number plate.

For the next seven minutes, he watched the car, as nothing happened.

He wondered what he should do: wake Britt, who was the least likely to do something stupid; or Catherine, who would know what to do, even if it was? In the end, he decided Molly would want him to check it out himself. He knew his Mother would hate that, thus making it the heroic thing to do.

He went down the stairs, past the bedroom where he could hear Britt breathing in her sleep. He opened the back door without a sound. Outside it was only marginally cooler than inside. The night was still. He crossed to the fence, only to find he couldn't open the side gate.

He re-entered the house through to the back door, which he opened, more or less silently. A small bump made him pause, but there was no other sound. He moved towards the front of the house, wincing as the gravel of the driveway let him know how soft his feet were.

Someone was inside the car. The figure was large, making Boris suspect it was male, or a large woman. It was definitely the car they had seen earlier. He checked the number plate, noting he had made it out correctly before. He crept forward.

The person inside stirred and Boris suddenly tasted bile in his mouth, wondering too late about guns and knives.

The car door opened. Boris wished he'd put on his boots. He lurched forward and yelled, deciding attack was the best form of defence.

As he came to the vehicle, the door slammed and the car started. Boris put a hand on the passenger side windscreen, and pushed his face against the foggy glass. The horn blared, and the car jolted forward, lifting Boris and dropping him back on his arse on the grassy curb. The engine belched, then roared. For the second time in three hours, he watched the car's tail lights disappear around a corner.

A dog started barking on the other side of the road.

Boris was breathing deeply as Catherine appeared in a maroon dressing gown. She looked down at Boris. 'What the hell, man? Are you trying to drum up some trade?'

He accepted her offered hand. Britt appeared behind her.

'Same car as before. He was just parked here.'

Britt clicked her tongue. 'Why didn't you wake me?'

Boris put a hand on his chest. He was aware of the sweat on his face. 'I had the feeling if I woke you, it would turn out to be nothing.'

Britt nodded. 'It's a kind of logic. What did you see?'

They went up the stairs; there was no sign of Andy. Boris kept his voice low. 'I got the number plate down on the newspaper in there.' He gestured to the sunroom. 'I didn't see much, but I'm pretty sure he's male and big.'

Catherine put the kettle on. 'That's a fair chunk of the population.'

Britt rubbed her nose. 'Catherine, are you sure you haven't annoyed someone? Perhaps at that Greens thing?'

'I don't think so, and all the men there were whippet thin. I suspect if they were stalking us, it would at least be in a Prius.'

'Or an ebike.' Boris smirked. 'What about the weird bloke who talked to you on the beach?'

Catherine turned the teapot three times clockwise as she thought about it. 'I don't think I annoyed him. Also, he'd be stone drunk by midday. He just said he liked me.'

'Maybe it's him then. You're getting all the male attention,' said Britt.

Catherine's eyes flashed. 'You can have that one, Detective. Oh Boris, you're bleeding.'

Boris turned his elbow. 'Shoot, I am.' He reached for a tissue and pressed it against the graze. 'If this is just a suitor, I'm not getting involved. You go on being attractive, I'll sleep.'

Britt accepted the tea Catherine passed her. 'Don't encourage her, dear.'

Catherine walked into the combined living and kitchen area the next morning, noticing the smell of coffee in the air and two strange sounds. One was Boris snoring on the couch, where he had dozed off after the excitement of last night. The other had a tone somewhere between the tap of a woodpecker and the scratch of a quill on parchment. The rhythm of it was far too methodical for this time of the morning. Such sounds were only acceptable in the afternoon, to Catherine's way of thinking, and never on a holiday.

Britt sat at the generous varnished bench with a steaming mug beside her and an A4 notepad in front of her. She was using her pen violently: the source of the mystery noise.

Oblivious to any sounds, Andy could be seen in the sunroom doing some form of yoga. Catherine silently saluted his commitment to downward facing dogs and poured a still warm coffee from the jug.

She added milk and glanced at Britt's work. On the pad were two sketches: one of a familiar body and one of either a badly drawn slingshot or a precisely drawn stab wound, which was also familiar.

'Britt?' she asked quietly. 'Have you woken up a psychopath, by any chance?'

Britt didn't look up from her drawing. 'I don't think so, but I am a little preoccupied.' She spun the pad to face Catherine. 'Are these accurate in regard to the corpse of Brandon Miles-Barclay?'

Catherine took a meditative sip and thought about either microwaving the coffee or making a fresh pot. Britt saying things like "in regard to" were threatening her precarious morning mood, but she tried to find it amusing. 'The body had more clothes. But the stab wound is eerily similar.'

'I deliberately left out the clothes.'

'You're in a bad frame of mind. Perhaps we should go down to the surf lifesaving club today?'

'Shush Catherine. You're not helping anyone.' She studied her drawings. 'I'm by no means a doctor. But look at this.' She revealed a large encyclopaedia beside her that she must have found in the accommodation's library downstairs. When she opened a page, Catherine clicked her tongue. The medical representation of a male body, minus skin and showing muscle and organs greeted her. Britt pointed to the subject's abdomen. 'I don't think that stab wound would have killed him. Not immediately.'

Catherine studied the page. 'What's your theory?'

'So far, just a theory. I don't think he died and then was swept out to sea. I think he was either stabbed in the water and couldn't get out and drowned or bled out. Or he was in a boat when he was stabbed and was tossed in the water.'

'That's lots of theories.'

Britt's grin was entirely too bright for the morning. Catherine took another sip and decided she was going to have to make a fresh pot. This lukewarm coffee was substandard for a holiday experience. She tipped the coffee into the sink and cleared her throat quietly. 'When did this come to you?'

'I woke up thinking about it. Don't you wake up thinking about solutions to a problem?'

Catherine had to concede the point and she filled the kettle.

Andy walked in. 'Thirty-four degrees today. That's the kind of weather I tell everyone back in Fife about and they think I'm on Mars.'

Britt passed him the encyclopaedia. 'Page 42, mate. Get your planetary geography up to date.'

Andy smiled, and his eyes raised, the way they often did when he was thinking, as if the answers were written on the inside of his eyebrows. 'Did I say Mars? Sorry, Mercury. Mars would be more like mid-winter Scotland. Take the red away for a lovely eternal grey.'

Catherine scooped coffee grounds. 'How are you always so cheerful then?'

'A Scotsman's rebellious nature. Want me to be on your team for volleyball today, Britt? Even the odds against Catherine.'

Britt's eyes narrowed. 'She cheated.' She ignored Catherine's innocent smile.

Andy gestured to their sleeping friend on the couch, eyes still closed. 'Then she gets Boris as a penance.'

'I'm no penance,' came Boris's gruff voice from the couch. 'I'm ninety kilos of raw power.'

'Two false statements.' Catherine flicked the kettle on. 'It's about eighty-five, and not so much raw as unpolished.'

Britt stood up, sheepishly bold. 'I need to make a phone call.'

'That's okay,' said Andy. 'You're allowed a phone. Why are you announcing it?'

Catherine found sugar for Boris on the bench. 'I suspect Britt is momentarily going on the clock.'

Britt raised two hands. 'It won't take long. I swear. Give me half an hour and I will be relaxed, and you will be getting thrashed at volleyball.'

She gestured to the large windows in the sunroom, which gave a view of the beach, less than a kilometre away. The water twinkled flirtatiously.

'Go get it done. Boris won't be match fit before a plate of something greasy anyway.' Boris made a satisfied snuffling sound into his mug. 'Once he's finished making us breakfast, I'm sure you'll know that the case is fine without you.'

Britt exhaled. 'I can't believe Thomas didn't come and see us. If he'd found the body on holiday, I would have had him fully debriefed.'

'Yes, but Thomas probably believes in holidays. Make the call downstairs. Your work voice will kill my mood.'

'Shan't be long,' Britt called as she moved down the stairs.

'If you're not there by midday, you have to bring champagne,' Catherine called after her.

Boris started rummaging in the cupboards for a frying pan. Andy sat heavily on the couch. 'I don't like champagne.'

'Don't worry, dear. I like it enough for both of us.'

As far as great sporting moments go, the antics of Boris, Andy and Catherine were probably not going to bother the history books, but when Britt joined them an hour later, she was impressed by the level of sound with which they threw themselves into the volleyball. If a holiday can be judged by volume, they were going first class.

Catherine saw Britt coming but was concentrating on the ball. It accelerated towards the earth as if the planet had insulted it. Her feet pounded the sand as she realised that she was going to have to leap.

'I trust the sand won't hurt me' she murmured as her outstretched hands found the ball and punched it over her head. As the soft sand caught her a second after, she turned her head, just in time to see Boris spike the ball into Andy's far corner.

Catherine let out a barbaric yelp and waited for Boris to help her up. As she came upright, she called towards her approaching friend.

'That was an hour; you'd better be packing some Chandon.'

Britt slowed, and Catherine noticed she was wearing street clothes rather than a bathing suit. This was bad. She called to Andy who was poised to serve. 'You two stay warm. I'm taking a break.'

As she got close to Britt, she saw a certain smile that Britt only employed when she was extremely angry.

'How did that go?'

Her eye flickered. 'Oh, not great.'

'Is he reporting you to Williams as we speak?'

'No, not quite that bad. I wasn't sure what was worse though. What he wouldn't hear or what he told me.'

'What wouldn't he hear?'

'Well, as usual, a woman's voice. But specifically, he doesn't want to know about the stab wound not being lethal, factional stuff in the Greens and any views I may or may not have on the corpse.'

'What did he tell you?'

'Eventually, to shut up. But he reckons he's got it all sewn up, or close. That said, he let slip there is no suspect still in custody.

'So, Kayla's dad is out. What was he called? Barker?'

'He's called Travis Barker. Kayla was telling the truth. He hasn't been out of prison long.' She looked toward the sea. 'That's enough for a cop like Thomas.'

'Kayla was sure he wasn't involved.'

'You'd say that about your dad. So would I.'

Catherine gestured at the net. 'Ok. So, can we play volleyball and get drunk now, please?'

'Hmm.' Britt's face scrunched up. 'I can't ignore it. I just want to check a few leads. Thomas won't like talking to people at the Greens HQ.'

'Did you bring the champagne?'

'Nup.'

'Then we have to go into town anyway, to get that.' She turned to Andy and Boris, who were between points. 'Hey, fellas. We're going to town.'

Andy bounced the ball and began walking over. 'Why do I have the distinct feeling you're not offering to buy the lunchtime chips?'

Catherine smiled indulgently. 'Still high on the agenda. We just have to solve a problem before Britt can go back to holiday mode.'

'The body?'

Britt nodded. 'It's part of the problem, yes.'

Andy exhaled through his nostrils. 'Can I point out that this is Australia and we have a perfectly competent police force?'

Britt was deadpan. 'I know them better than you.'

Andy pointed a finger. 'That's unfair.'

'Yes, it is. Shall I arrest myself with my super competency?'

'No.' Andy looked away, then back. 'Fine. Do the Miss Marple routine. Just don't get me involved this time. I'm still recovering from the last trauma.'

Britt cleared her throat. 'You mean when I got kidnapped?'

Boris added. 'And me?'

'And my boyfriend died?' Catherine's voice was lighter than most peoples would have been.

Andy's voice was high. 'Well, when you put it that way, I ah…' He bounced the ball in frustration. 'You know last time I went away with people, they were talking about real estate the whole time and I was bored. Now I'm away with you guys and it's all skulduggery. Surely there's a middle ground, eh?'

Boris clapped him on the back. 'Don't worry, the universe is a great leveller.'

Catherine laughed as Andy sighed. 'Don't worry. We'll leave you Boris for now.'

'Yeah, but I can tell he's all in.'

Boris shrugged. 'Come on. If we focus on something else, no one will notice me sulking occasionally. Let's leave them to it. We'll swim and then get some chips. I'll buy you a lunchtime pint.'

Andy's face made several small contortions as he tried in vain to find something about this he could argue against. Catherine and Britt had walked off before he finished.

'I honestly don't know how they could make it this hard.'

Britt was glaring at her phone, as she had been for the past twelve minutes. 'Hmm.'

'Why don't they just put the address on their website? Don't they want people to come and shower them with money?' Catherine looked down at her heel, which she suspected was developing a blister from her new sandals. She was almost as annoyed by her footwear as she was proud of the winter grey broad brim hat she was wearing. One of her recent presents to herself. If the day was going to be interrupted with police work, she was at least going to look fabulous.

'You can do that online.'

'Online.' Catherine threw her hands up. 'Everything's online. Even political donations.'

Britt didn't look up from her phone search. 'Aren't your hats online?'

'Yes, but so is my address. People can shower me with cash in person anytime.'

Britt grunted, 'It sounds different when you say it about you. I could call?'

'Who, Williams? Tell him you've become a socialist?'

'Here we go.' She walked ahead, towards a man with a hessian backpack, walking a greyhound.

Christ, thought Catherine, don't go cop. Don't interrogate. She kicked off her sandals to catch up, only to hear her friend sound oddly gentle.

'Hi, are you flyering for the Greens?'

He stopped, a broad smile on his face. 'I am. Without a candidate, of course, but the cause is just.'

'Right.' Britt beamed in a way Catherine had never seen before. 'Hey, my friend and I are down to flyer too, but I lost his number.'

The man gently placed a flyer with Brandon Miles-Barclay on it into a yellow post box. 'Whose number?'

'Oh, I can't even remember his name, but he's really nice and has a beard.'

Catherine stood amazed at Britt's act.

The man's face lit up. 'Raheem?'

'That's it.' Britt almost snapped her fingers. 'It was Raheem, Catherine. Right?'

'Sure.'

The man fished out his phone as he walked. 'I've got his number.'

Britt walked with him. 'Oh, just let us know where we pick up the flyers from.'

'HQ is on the main drag, three doors down from the Ming Terrace. I can't remember the number. Raheem's there now.'

Britt beamed. 'Thanks a million.'

He gave the peace sign before taking his greyhound further down the street.

Catherine grimaced as she now stood on a stick in her bare and blistered feet. 'That was amazing,' she said through the sting.

'It's not always a badge that works.'

'I guessed that, but I've never seen you lie like that. And I believed it. I thought we were down here to volunteer as well.'

'Don't get too cute, Catherine. It wasn't amazing. It's what you do. You've just never seen anyone else do it.'

'Am I that good?'

'Probably not.'

Fifteen minutes later, they were at Greens HQ. It looked like it was usually a clothes shop, more on the scale of high fashion than hemp clothing and Rastafarian tee shirts. Today, it was a hive of activity. Phones were glued to everyone's ear while a man with a beard pushed flyers and photocopied maps with streets highlighted for letterboxing into the hands of young people.

Six people sat at desks typing. Catherine, still angry at how long it had taken to find the place, assumed they were encrypting new ways of not giving up their address. Beyond them, a man talked to two women. All of them held coffees and he was somehow sawing the air with his hand and rolling a cigarette at the same time.

'Hi, can I help?' A familiar woman with plaited hair approached them. Catherine remembered her from the beach yesterday.

'Hello, you're Shelby, aren't you? I'm Catherine. This is Britt. We came to see how a campaign was run.'

Shelby smiled. 'This could be an approximation. Are you here to volunteer?'

'We're thinking about it.' Britt started. 'We're here on holiday, but after the death…'

'The murder.' Shelby was firm.

Catherine vocally backpedalled. 'Yeah.'

Shelby's mouth pursed briefly before she spoke again. 'It starts with a broken window. It happens at least once a campaign. People are angry. I've never seen it go this far in Australia.'

Britt's hand touched the counter. 'Was there a previous threat?'

'A man broke a window. I believe he was arrested the day of the murder.'

'Travis Barker.'

'That's his name.' She paused. 'I'm all about due process. Let the courts find out.' Her brow knitted. 'How do you know his name? Journos?'

Britt was quick. 'I heard it in the café this morning. How is everyone holding up?'

'We're okay. It's so horrible. We'll mourn after the 8th.'

Catherine stepped in. 'That's still four weeks away. Is there talk of a new candidate?'

'We're getting close.' She blushed. 'We're negotiating with the electoral commission for an extension on nomination time. So, you want some flyers? We're pretty busy. I'm sorry, no time for tourists.' She passed them two bundles of leaflets. 'You can do the supermarket.'

'Great.' Catherine took them. 'Just one more thing. How was Brandon polling?'

Shelby's voice was low. 'Third. A strong third. But he was the kind of guy that was going to grow and grow. The number of volunteers pouring in is amazing.'

'Hard to win from third, though.' Though not impossible, with the preferential voting system.

Shelby nodded. 'Especially preaching equality around here. That doesn't mean we won't fight for it.'

'Shit.' Britt suddenly gripped Catherine's upper arm, hard. Catherine followed her gaze to Ocean Grove's busy main street. Two people were walking fast in their direction. Their posture was zero per cent fear and fifteen per cent resentment. Cops. One of them had a terrible moustache.

Catherine rubbed her shoulder: Britt was cutting off her circulation. 'Oh, goodness. Thanks Shelby. We'll be around. Is there a back way out?'

Shelby blinked twice. 'Ah, it's for campaign staff only.'

Britt's whisper was high pitched. 'He mustn't see me.'

Catherine smiled at Shelby. 'Okay. Bye. Peace in our time.'

Britt increased the pressure of her grip. 'Catherine.'

They had eight seconds before the cops walked in the door. If Catherine and Britt left now, they would run straight into them.

Catherine led her stricken friend towards the door and then to a nearby wall. As they moved, Catherine put her grey broad brim on Britt's head. Once at the wall, Catherine leaned back against it, and held Britt's neck. Moved her closer.

Britt practically whimpered. 'This won't do. They'll see me.'

'Pucker up.' Catherine then pulled Britt's mouth against hers, pushing her body towards the door. Britt stiffened, then relaxed as she realised the ruse.

When Thomas and Perfetto came in, they had to sidestep the snogging women, one face completely obscured by a grey hat, just inside the Greens HQ.

'Jesus, excuse us, ladies,' came Thomas' voice as he raised his arms to pass. Perfetto sidestepped easily. This gave Catherine and Britt the six seconds they needed to break their smooch and move through the door.

They made a hard left to get beyond the eyes in the window within a half second of leaving.

Within thirty seconds they were around the nearest corner. Catherine in fits of hysterical laughter, Britt simply shaking.

'How was that? Am I good on my feet or what?' Catherine hooted.

'You're a mad woman!' Britt was still wiping Catherine's lips gloss from her mouth. 'That could have gone spectacularly badly. What if they had seen me do that?'

Catherine held her stomach which was beginning to ache. 'You're on holidays, do what you like.'

'What I like? Have you ever?' Britt let off an expletive loud enough for a nearby seagull to take flight.

Catherine went on chuckling.

'He only bloody went there because I mentioned it. Maybe Perfetto convinced him.' Britt leaned on a wooden fence. After a breath, she glared at Catherine, flushed. 'I could see the faces in the room. Almost everyone was looking at us.'

Catherine was metaphorically picking herself up off the ground. 'If we'd been at a Liberal HQ, they'd have maced us. Oh.' She sniffed. 'Wow. Nice one. Hey, pass me my hat.'

Britt threw it, her lips pursed to the point of being colourless. 'I don't think we even found out anything.'

Catherine breathed deeply, trying to get her pulse rate down. 'Oh, don't be grumpy. We found out plenty.'

'That the candidate was polling third. I could have told you that without getting out of bed.'

Catherine wiped her eyes, before giving another round of throaty laughter. 'But he had so much energy.'

'They all do.' She stared at the two piles of leaflets in her hand. She swore as she hurled them into a bin.

'Brittney Houden.' Catherine chided. 'Don't you care about the planet?'

Britt swore again as she took them out of the bin and placed them gently in the recycling bin next to it. 'Okay?'

'Britt.' Catherine looked her friend in the eye. 'Are you upset, because you...' she smiled... 'felt something, back there?'

She held on for a full three seconds before she was pealing with laughter again.

Britt walked away. 'Oh, Christ, will you just...?'

'All right. Hey, you know what. We should go back and see what they're saying.'

'What?'

'We should see what Thomas and Perfetto are saying.'

'But I work with them. I just kissed you to stop them from noticing me.'

'Good point. I should go back and listen. You should go pick us up a coffee from that café over there and I'll meet you back here in fifteen.

Britt made four noises like a wombat trying to pronounce French, and then starting for the café. Catherine wondered if she'd gone too far.

Britt turned her head slightly. 'Don't screw it up!'

Catherine smiled. We're good.

6

I don't know why anyone would walk on water if they could turn it into wine.

~ Catherine Kint

Catherine walked back to the crowd on the main street, which was dominated by the loud colours of current fashion. She had devised a plan. Returning to Greens HQ as the phantom smoocher would prove stupid, so she positioned herself on the opposite side of the street. She was ostensibly window shopping, looking at an antique spinning wheel that was going for a bargain price that would buy you a pretty decent car. After a few minutes, two familiar figures exited the Greens HQ.

Thomas was short and solid, and, Catherine now noticed, had an ironic mullet, *en vogue* even in police circles. Selena Perfetto was half a head taller than him. She was staring at her phone and shaking her head. They stood out from the crowd by wearing full-length pants and shirts in a crowd of people in shorts, loose tops and tee shirts. They started towards the east side of the street, towards the post office – and the Zebra bar.

She followed at a distance before coming to the obvious conclusion that she'd have to get closer if she wanted to hear what they were saying. She decided to walk past them and listen, then fiddle with her shoe, hearing another five seconds or so. Having a now fully formed blister would make it more plausible. All she had to do was put her sandals back on.

Catherine power-walked to two metres behind them. She heard Perfetto say, 'I'm not sure.' She was distracted when an exuberant, dimpled boy of about seven danced into her, part of a throng of children bopping to a Rolling Stones song outside a café. A bearded man wearing a ridiculous Hawaiian shirt waved at her. 'Sorry, sister.' Then, to the child, 'Take it easy, Macca.'

Catherine smiled icily at the goofball hippy and kept walking, her blister hurting more convincingly than needed. As she closed in, she deliberately looked well past her targets.

Thomas' voice was gruff but even. 'They're not going to kick up a stink. I think we use Occam's Razor on this.'

'The least assumptions?'

'The easiest way.'

'I'm not convinced. And that's not what Occam's Razor is. What about the woman on CCTV?'

Thomas snorted. 'There were lots of women on the CCTV.'

Catherine walked past.

'How many were carrying a knife?' Perfetto was clearly annoyed.

Catherine dropped to her haunches and pulled a convincing "Oh no, my foot has a blister" face. She heard Thomas reply, 'Let's just watch the bad guy. You'll learn.'

Catherine rolled her eyes and decided for the eight millionth time that leaving the force was the best thing she'd ever done. She couldn't make out exactly what Perfetto's reply was, but the tone was not acquiescent.

Catherine would lobby Britt to form an allegiance with this woman. She had potential.

Catherine's right foot was now in a state of quiet agony. It would need a stiff dose of medicine very soon, with lime. Or at least a band-aid. She made a beeline for the chemist then took her time walking back down the street, enjoying the warm red bricks under her feet. Life was good. The dancing kids were still going strong, with Dimples shaking his butt for all it was worth to *Start Me Up*. Catherine grinned; she been started for hours.

A few minutes later, Catherine was holding her sandals in one hand and the worst coffee in human history in the other. 'I swear you're getting back at me.'

'Don't be ridiculous.' Britt's brow was furrowed as she took a sparrow sip from her own steaming cardboard cup.

They left the main street to cut through the supermarket. Catherine caught sight of Kayla, sitting by a group of teenagers. Catherine gave a wave and was surprised to have it returned.

'Is your coffee okay?' Catherine was bordering on shrill and she knew it.

'It's fine.' Britt smiled at the man in the red shirt who passed her an Australian Labor Party flyer, which she took neutrally. 'Maybe milliners have higher expectations of their mid-morning beverages than cops. I swear I asked for your usual. The barista even had a cool haircut.'

Catherine groaned, waving away the pamphlet offered to her. 'That should have been a warning. If coffee came in a cask, it would taste like this.'

They were halfway back to their rented house. The sun was bright, and the ferny trees were dipping low over the grassed paths. The traffic in these streets seemed low, almost ridiculously so with the main streets so busy. Catherine could hear magpies warbling and the buzz of insects.

'Tell me again what they said?'

Catherine blinked, wincing as she stood on a small stone. 'Oh, he was all' she put on a gruff gangster voice. '"It's an open and shut case, sugar. Now roll me a cigarette while you fall in love with me".'

Britt snorted.

'Perfetto seemed completely human, seeing a bigger picture and not hiding that she thinks he's a prick.' She ducked a branch. 'Honestly, she gets my vote. She can come to dinner, I'm sure she has excellent politics.' She took a few more steps as a thought came to her. 'Hey?'

'Hey what?'

'How many cops do you know who vote Green?'

'None, but probably because I don't talk about it.'

'Who do cops vote for?'

'Whoever we want. We get more pay from Labor, more trust from the Libs. Who cares?'

Catherine kept sipping. Maybe it wasn't quite so bad. 'Just wondering why cops don't like Greens.'

Britt almost snarled, 'Probably because we're mostly working class.'

Catherine was stunned for a few seconds. 'That was heartfelt.' She said brightly.

'I always look up the candidates before election day.' Britt finished her coffee. She grimaced cheerfully, which Catherine understood as cop for an apology. 'I'm having a cold feet moment. Sitting on the beach beating Boris at volleyball sounds good right now.'

Catherine exhaled loudly. 'So before, when I was ready to crack champagne, you wanted to go to work, but now that we know something is up, you want to go to the beach?'

'I'm a complicated woman.'

'I want to see what the other parties are saying about the murder. Plus, I want to know when big Mr Barker got out of a cell and if it was him playing chicken with us up the road last night.' Catherine grabbed the flyer in Britt's hand. 'How's this? We'll see the boys and organise lunch. This afternoon, we send Boris to look at the ALP dudes, check the Liberals later and if there's nothing, we can both consider our itches scratched.'

'Not all of them.'

Catherine snorted. 'Well, I'm sure Andy will love hanging around the lifesaving club.'

Britt rolled her eyes, then brought out her phone, which had chirped. Britt seemed even less impressed.

'What?'

'The number plate on that car.'

Catherine stepped up eagerly. 'Yeah?'

'It belongs to a seventy-year-old female artist in the northern suburbs of Melbourne.'

'Stolen?'

'My mate called her. She could see the car while they were talking.'

Catherine's mouth made an O. 'Boris took down the wrong number.'

'Amateurs.'

Catherine held out a hand, consoling. 'He's on holiday.'

With her friends' fish and chip orders in her back-pocket, Catherine made her way along the beach route to the town. She could probably let all the intrigue go if it weren't for the car incident last night. Not that she was particularly scared, but when someone parks outside your house in the middle of the night, you want to know why. Generally speaking, she didn't warrant that much interest from the general public; hence, she was curious.

The beach closest to town was teeming with life. Young children, teenagers, parents, and grandparents all enjoying the heat and the water.

The crowd was concentrated between the two yellow and red flags, marking where the lifesavers patrolled. Catherine was keeping an eye out for the large man, Golledge, from yesterday, wondering if he was a beach regular and if he still considered her lucky.

She was also wondering if Duc was on beach patrol and might be enticed to take a quick break.

She moved off the sand and came upon a strip of picnic tables. Two men in blue singlets and expensive sneakers sat at one of them, watching the beach, passing a large cigarette and drinking premixed drinks in black cans. They looked up as she came along the path.

'You're Travis Barker,' she said.

The big man bristled. He had a large bandage on his left lower arm. 'Who wants to know?'

'I'm Catherine. I hear you're in trouble.'

His head shifted. Even with the sunnies on, he obviously wasn't looking at her. 'Only one of us is in trouble. Make it none by walking away.'

'I could help you.'

'I don't know you. Walk away. Now.' His tone brooked no argument, but Catherine lingered. He was more powerfully built than Catherine had realised. All upper body too, no beer belly, despite the midday can in front of him. His companion was the same rat-faced man who had been with Barker the night he was arrested. He sucked hard on the joint – Catherine could smell it now – and stared at her. The hair on her neck stood up. She kept walking.

Some people can, even without speaking, make you feel like going home and never going out again. They're the type of people that are used by both sides of politics to scare people into their tribe. Barker's mate was one of them. Not so much deliberately scary as effortlessly cold and as indifferent as nature, and enough to make you hate nature, even on a sunny day.

The fish shop was busy with people, mostly children. While it made sense for one adult to do the lunch run (as Catherine had done for her friends) many in the town seemed to think that there was no way to bond better than waiting in irritated silence or whiny conversation at the local fish and chippery.

Catherine, when she found her order would be a twenty-minute wait, decided that even if she'd been in a minefield with a live volcano erupting, instead of a lovely seaside village, she would wait outside rather than endure the vocal chorus of a hundred angry families.

She walked down the main drag, enjoying the secure band-aid protection over her blister and the warm sun on her skin. As she passed the supermarket, she was surprised by a gentle tugging at her elbow.

Kayla was sitting on the bench again. Her eyes were mascaraed up, part racoon, part young woman. She didn't say anything. Catherine lowered herself onto the bench beside her.

'Hi.'

Kayla smiled wanly as she stared at the black half-gloves she was wearing. Catherine thought it an odd choice, given the weather. But she remembered being a teenager enough to know that weather wasn't always important.

'How's your holiday?' Kayla asked.

'Good.'

'Some people don't think you're on holiday.'

Catherine was aware that these racoony eyes were trying to pierce hers. 'Why's that?'

'You've been asking questions.'

'That's how you get to know a place. Elementary tourism, really. I see your dad's back out. That's good.'

Kayla cracked her right forefinger knuckle with the thumb of the same hand. 'I can't see him.'

'Your Mum?'

'My stepdad. He's a shit.'

'Right.'

'You don't care about that.' She stared at her feet, sulking in the way teenagers have sulked for over a million years. Catherine thought the least she could do was not lie by saying she cared, so she maintained the silence. After a minute, Kayla spoke again. 'You know something, don't you?'

Catherine chose her words carefully. 'I don't; only that there's something to know. What do you know?'

Kayla grimaced. 'Same as you. Something's wrong.' She nodded back towards the supermarket. 'Mum's acting strange and Jim's worse than usual. That's saying something.'

'Your stepdad?'

'Yep.' She turned back to Catherine. 'Someone knows something about the dead fag. I think the cops will just go back to Dad. You're not a cop, are you?'

'No, never was.'

'Cops want to get a job done. I think you want to find something out.'

Catherine swallowed. This seemed like a set-up. 'What do you want Kayla?'

'I want you to find out. I want my Mum to stop being scared. That's all.'

'I'll do what I can.' She pointed towards the chip shop. 'Gotta go.'

'Bye.'

Catherine was four steps away when Kayla called out, 'If I can help, tell me.'

Catherine gave her a half-smile. All around the street were children of different ages, just being kids. 'Sure.'

Eight minutes later, Catherine walked down the beach path again. She had thought of taking the other way to her friends, but didn't want one poor interaction with Barker and his companion to put her off walking anywhere. They had gone anyway, leaving the two empty tinnies on the concrete picnic tables. Catherine put the chips down and picked up their litter. A small act to make the world better. Keep doing the little things, she thought to herself.

'It's just about doing the little things right. Keeping the workers at the forefront of your mind and making sure that the middle class isn't left behind by big money.' The man was Boris in ten years, or could be. Middle-aged, broad and hirsute. He spoke incessantly and urgently. Boris, a barman of many years, had to fight the urge to pour him a pint, his usual escape from such men.

About four metres away, Britt was in a similar discussion with a young, dark-skinned woman, who was pushing home the points in five directions for her audience.

Boris could see that Labor thought they had a chance in the election and were pushing for all their worth. There was no sign of the candidate, whom Boris now knew was a local unionist who had fought hard through Geelong's decline as a car manufacturing city. Boris could only have picked her out of the crowd due to the massive posters that dominated the main street.

Boris cleared his throat during a miniscule pause in the conversation.

'Hey, mate, what about the murder the other day? How do you think that changes things?'

The Labor man, who had introduced himself as Alan or Dave – Boris couldn't remember – sucked in his cheeks and gave a sombre nod. 'It's a tragedy for his family and his community, but I don't see how it changes the by-election. Put simply, and I say this with great respect, the bloke who was going to come third, won't.'

'So, you're not breathing a sigh of relief.'

'Ah,' he scratched his head. 'No. If he'd made a misstep and was politically dead maybe, but he's actually dead, so I can't say I have any good feelings about it.'

'I've heard it's been a bit heated among the volunteers.'

'Not that heated. Plus, just in case you're indicating anything, we were launching our campaign in Torquay that night.'

'Nah mate. I'm sorry. I'm just curious.' Boris, well versed in how to act sheepishly, had both his hands up. 'I didn't mean that. I know it's a tough game, but not that.'

Alan/Dave continued. 'They were gonna hit us hard on the Spring Creek thing, but we were ready.'

Boris tried to sound upbeat. 'The Spring Creek thing?'

'Yeah. They want to push that we don't listen to the electorate, but it was our Minister who blocked it and at least one of their councillors voted for it in the surf coast shire, when they agreed to offsets using yellow gums. Inconsistent, see?'

'Right. So, it's a big issue down here?'

The chap blinked. Boris thought he knew why. 'Down here? Where did you say you were from mate?'

'Brunswick.'

'Right, excuse me.' He moved past to find someone local.

Boris shrugged and walked to the refreshments stall to pay more than he usually would for a can of local lager.

'Love one,' came Britt's voice as he pocketed his change. He caught the barman just in time for a second. He almost complained, but the memory of the misread number plate was fresh in both their minds.

He passed the tinnie to Britt and they moved further away from the madding crowd.

'Wasn't them.' Boris started.

'Nup. Campaign launch.'

'Unless it was a full assassination.'

'Not with that knife. I've seen stab wounds like that in suburban kitchens.'

'I don't know. They seem pretty organised.'

'This beer is perfectly cold.'

He held the can like a holy relic. 'Wonderfully.'

'I almost feel I'm on holiday.'

'Almost.'

Britt reached for the phone beeping in her pocket. Boris watched as she read the text. Had it been anyone else, he would have assumed it was a romantic thing. She smiled thoughtfully.

'That was work, wasn't it?'

He liked that she didn't seem guilty about it. 'Yep. After this morning's call to Thomas, I asked one of the other homicide detectives how he was going. Apparently, they found nothing of interest at the victim's house.'

'Which makes you think?'

'Usually, I would say it means there was nothing of interest. But in this case, I would say it's because they didn't want to find anything.'

Her phone buzzed again in her hand. This time she frowned.

'Problem?' asked Boris.

'No. That one was from Andy. Apparently, he only gets four weeks' holiday a year and is wondering when we can play more volleyball. He sent it to you too. And Catherine.'

Boris rolled his eyes. 'Shall I tell him to play with himself, or is that funnier from you?'

Again, the phone buzzed. Britt laughed. 'Catherine just said that. You two hang out together too much.'

'You sound like Molly.'

'Sorry that didn't work out.'

Boris sighed. 'Me too.' His beer was almost empty. 'You think I can get one more before they call time?'

Britt nodded. 'I reckon, but stop after two beers.'

Boris raised an eyebrow as he sipped.

'I think I want you to break into Brandon's place tonight.'

Boris spat beer and narrowly missed spraying a woman in a red ALP tee shirt. Britt bought him the second can by way of apology.

7

The sea is death, dancing nearer then further, always there.
It will be there when you're gone too.

~ Sean Golledge

'But it's illegal!' Andy's voice was strained to the point of screaming. He had entered a sonic zone known as "whiny" some minutes earlier and was escalating. He pointed at Britt. 'She can confirm it. You would be breaking and entering, trespassing and interfering with a police investigation.' He grabbed air with his hands. 'Generally, not being on holiday.'

Britt surveyed the scene: the Scotsman was getting more and more worked up about not relaxing enough while standing in front of the overstuffed bookshelves. After Catherine had made it clear it was her idea – to make him like it – he had completely ignored Boris and Britt and was focusing all his rage on Catherine. After a few minutes Boris had picked up a book. Britt was tempted to do the same, but she was invested in the discussion.

'Andy, really. You've made a few points.' Catherine was desperately trying not to laugh. 'First, we are on holiday, where you get to do what you like. Second, what we feel like doing is having a look at Brandon Miles-Barclay's house. And third, we've been toeing around the police investigation all day and it would seem a shame to back out now. I've suffered. I had to kiss Britt.'

'This is the limit,' Andy replied, not realising that Catherine had started counting the seconds on her fingers. 'I come down for some well-earned R and-' His eyes widened; his voice dropped. 'What did you say?'

'I got to four. You were really committed to yelling.'

'You kissed Britt?'

Boris audibly snapped his book closed. 'Really?'

Britt stared at her shoes. 'It was just a way of not getting noticed. Under' – she paused – 'cover.'

'Not noticed, by kissing? I'm suddenly all ears.' Boris looked from Britt to Catherine, who was almost luminous with glee.

'She won't talk, Boris, but trust me, she's changed.'

Britt cleared her throat. 'If we could get back to the plan, Andy was arguing that we should just have a movie night.'

Catherine placed her palms on the table. 'Yes. But the rest of us think that one man has died, and another may get the blame due to being a big scary dude and the cops being lazy. I can't let that happen, even when we've got many, many, bad movies to watch.'

Andy slumped onto the green couch. 'So, it's hopeless. I can't stop you.'

'No, nor can you beat us. But you can join us.'

Andy rubbed his face. Britt chimed in. 'We could really use another pair of hands, and his house is only four blocks from here.'

Andy stood and marched to the fridge. His silhouette was dark against the fading light outside. He opened the fridge door, nodding. He picked up a lager and came back to the couch.

Catherine smiled. 'Dutch courage?'

Andy shook his head and took a long sip. 'No, I'm just making the best of it. There are eight cans of lager in that fridge, and, if I'm not mistaken, I saw a *Buffy the Vampire Slayer* Season Six box set over there. You guys can go and do what you need to. I'm going to be on holiday.' There was a finality to the statement.

Britt indicated they go downstairs to the second living space, which Britt was using as a bedroom. 'Let's give him some space so he can watch his soaps.'

'Not a soap!' Andy called.

Britt raised her eyebrows. 'Oh yeah, it's an ironically loveable study of humanity; with monsters as metaphor for the demons within us all. That's what you always said, right Boris?'

Boris chewed on this as he went down the stairs. 'Um, yeah I did.'

Downstairs, Britt plopped down onto her queen-size mattress as Boris and Catherine sat on the couch. Britt looked at Catherine. 'You're all in, suddenly.'

Catherine shrugged. 'I had another chat with Kayla. She seems perfectly messed up and I can't watch that follow its logical progression.'

'I don't want to be there,' Britt said suddenly.

Catherine was incredulous. 'At Miles-Barclay's? Did you not see how hard I fought for the idea up there?'

Britt crossed her arms. 'Yep. But if you guys get caught, there's a fine. I get caught, I lose everything. Sorry.'

Catherine made a noise that was half huff and half yodel.

Boris absent-mindedly cracked a knuckle. 'You'll pay my fine?'

'Sure. Plus, I saw there's a Liberal's thing out near the freeway. I could get dolled up and go to that. See what I can hear?'

Catherine hummed. 'I suppose you'd be doing me a favour. I doubt I could stand the crowd.'

Britt half swallowed a smirk. 'Yes, and no doubt you'd know more of them than me.'

Catherine eyes widened. 'Hey there, Madam hot-then-cold-then-tepid, this is no time to get snooty about class.'

Britt gave a painful smile. 'Sorry, you can blame that on my blue collar upbringing.'

Catherine's glare could've melted the rings of Saturn. 'Oh, for Christ's sake, you grew up in Blackburn. Don't go all Oliver Twist on me.'

Boris snuffled laughter. Britt took interest in her shoes. 'I know. I'm painfully aware that when you're not into it, all I want to do is the case. And then, when you want to do it, I can see it's madness. My Dad's so proud I made Detective.'

Catherine ran a hand through her hair. 'I say, if it makes you uncomfortable, it's a good idea. I really want to break in.' She turned to Boris. 'One for the road then off?'

'Deal.' Boris was already heading back up the stairs.

'He's a treasure, isn't he?'

Britt looked icy. 'Don't screw this up. I know it was my idea, but just, don't.'

They walked to the house, a one-storey affair on a small estate, two kilometres from the main town. The night was warm and alive with mozzies.

'So, you're sure he was single?' Boris checked as they did a walk-by.

'His website said as much. Also, Britt confirmed with her contact at homicide.'

Police tape was still evident on the doorway. It shifted slightly in the breeze. It was one of the few things that could be easily seen in the dim light of evening. Catherine and Boris walked halfway up the street, pretended to see something in the nature clearing that backed on to Miles Barclay's house in case someone was watching, before returning slowly to the front of the house. A car cruised past them, its white, sleek frame covered in the blue checks of the Victoria Police.

'That puts the wind up me a bit,' Boris murmured.

'I agree. Let's go around the block and think about it.'

'Is Britt's connection at homicide solid?'

'I imagine so. She's pretty picky who she trusts.'

'Let's have a look-out. I'll go in and you keep watch.' Boris indicated a large bush at the corner of the street. 'Pretend you're birdwatching or something.'

'Why you?'

'Because a small woman hanging out could be doing anything. Alone at night, I'm scarier.'

'Did you bring your headphones for the mobile trick?'

Boris checked his pocket and swore. 'No. Sorry.'

Catherine passed him hers. 'I can be on the phone looking for a dog.'

'Good one. Hope the dog's cute.' He was already walking away. He dialled her number.

'Check, check,' came Catherine's voice in his ear. 'Have you seen my dog?'

Boris pressed the earpiece in one ear. He found that filling both ears made him miss things. 'Okay, I'll tell you what I find.'

'We should have done this in the day.'

'Yeah. One day we'll get good at this.'

Boris entered the property and kept to the shadows as he moved to the back. Catherine knew not to talk unless he spoke or if she had to warn him. Boris's other ear and his eyes were on high alert for any sign of the law-abiding public, police, or, worse, an actual burglar.

The back garden was ill-kept, with native shrubs thriving under several giant paperbark trees. Good cover for a burglar, even if he was more of an errand boy.

The back door was locked. He knew he could get Catherine around to pick it, but he believed in luck and providence. The first two windows were stuck fast, but the third was a wind-out number. The hardest part was removing the flywire, but within minutes he was past it. He waited a full minute before he checked in with Catherine. 'I'm in.'

'I figured that. You stopped grunting a minute ago.'

'You're not exactly the voice to bring me confidence, are you?'

'Wait a sec.' Catherine's voice was serious. Boris froze.

After ten seconds, he whispered, 'What?'

'Oh, it's okay. I thought I saw someone who cared about your fragile confidence.'

Boris steadied himself on the window ledge as he exhaled and listened to her quietly cackle. 'In the morning, I'm going to poison your tea.'

'What do you see in there?'

'It's dark. I see that I'm in a dead man's house and it's dark.'

'Got your torch?'

'Yep. Tell me if you can see this.'

'Stop. Seriously, here comes a car.'

Boris's thumb twitched, but he hadn't pressed the button on his torch. He focused on the dark curtains of the bedroom he could see through the short hallway he occupied. They seemed closed, but he couldn't tell. He wished he'd checked before he came in. The car rumbled past and he heard Catherine exhale.

'Coast clear?'

'Yep.'

He switched on the hallway light. It shone through to the bedroom. On the side of the bedroom door was a waist-high plinth displaying a golden statue of a laughing Buddha. Boris patted the statue's head for luck then, remembering, he put his rubber gloves on and gave the deity's bonce a quick rub with his tee shirt.

The bedroom curtains were drawn. 'Can you see the light?'

'No.'

'Cool.'

He moved his torch slowly across the room. The bed was made. He wondered if it were Brandon's mother or a friend who had made it after the death, knowing he would never sleep in it again. Boris blessed himself, then, feeling ghoulish, he opened the bedroom drawer, knowing that some men keep their secrets close to where they sleep.

A familiar smell filled his nostrils, earthy and deep. 'Found some dope,' he reported. 'I don't think they even checked the bedroom.'

'Much?' Catherine spoke easily, at normal volume.

'A joint's worth. Strange, it's not in a bag.'

'Okay. Stop getting your entertainment in order. What else can you can see.'

'There's other stuff too. A powder, not white, and a couple of vials. One of them has Chinese writing on it.'

'What's it say?'

'It's in Chinese, Catherine. It could say "Carn the Bulldogs" and I wouldn't be any the wiser.'

'Take a photo of it on your phone. We can check it out later.'

'Good idea.' He took some snaps. A message appeared on his phone. "Memory card is full. These photos cannot be saved. You can manage your data in settings."

Boris swore.

'What?' Catherine was a mix of concerned and irritated.

'Nothing. I have to delete something.'

'Car.'

Boris stood completely still, staring at a clever painting of a bird's eye on the far wall. Again, he heard the coming and going of the cars. A rumble coming on, a whine leaving. He had never noticed how different a car sounded when it was getting closer than moving away. He was aware of sweat between his shoulder blades.

He forced his breath to slow and focused on what he was doing. Across the room, Boris slid the cupboard doors open. Shirts, pants, folded. Jumpers. A wetsuit in mint condition. On three rows of horizontal shelves there were tee shirts, books, and more books. Boris checked the far wall. Books there as well. Miles-Barclay was either well read or had meant to be. The third shelf down was out of alignment. He took a paperback down and shone his torch behind it. Something glinted. He took more books down and looked again. 'Oh ho.'

'What?'

Boris held the studded handcuffs in one hand and shone the torch on a small truncheon covered in small metal studs. 'Sex toys. Seems he lead a full life.'

'Okay. That doesn't make it right that someone stabbed him. See what else you can find.'

Boris gave a respectful nod to the handcuffs and replaced them, even returning the books. He hoped Brandon's family hadn't seen that, and quietly vowed to have a little clear-out when he got home. Just in case of mishap.

Boris moved into the lounge room.

After half an hour of being ignored, Britt wondered if she had lost her modelling edge, or whether the Liberal Party faithful were just not interested in meeting people they didn't regularly lunch with. She had read the bio on the back of Kathryn Cambridge's candidacy flyer three times in the past half hour. It was nice to know something about her. Catherine's only comment had been that she had spelt "Catherine" wrong.

After a career in financial law, said the bio, Cambridge was moved by the desire to improve the dialogue around welfare in the South Barwon district. She believed in hard work and had seen first-hand what it could do for young people. There were photos of her with local young people on the flyer. Nippers, horse riding and even a blue light disco, but for every one of these photos there were two of her with a grey-haired man. Several were elders of the community; one of them was the current Prime Minister. Either way, Britt couldn't help but think that her views on welfare and youth came more from these grey-haired men than people on welfare themselves.

A man in his forties in a decent suit approached her. 'Hello,' he started. 'I'm sorry, but did you work on the Indy campaign last Easter?'

'No, I'm a cop. I just wanted to come and support.'

'Oh.' He smiled, gracious in being wrong. 'That's nice. I'm sorry. I thought we'd worked together. Ant Carmichael.'

'Britt Houden.'

'Sergeant?'

'I'm on holiday.' She smiled, flattered that he was trying to flatter her.

'Right. Senior Constable?'

'Detective, actually. Homicide.' She enjoyed watching the flicker of surprise on his face, like watching a glass ceiling wobble.

'I see.' He recovered. 'Terrible business here the other day.'

'Miles-Barclay? Yes. You knew him?'

'I did. I work for the party out of Geelong, so we'd met several times. Decent fellow. We didn't agree on much, but decent.'

'Did he have any enemies, outside the norm?'

'Are you asking professionally?'

She laughed and touched his arm. 'Only out of professional interest. This isn't a sting on you, Ant.'

'Would you care for a wine?'

'Sure.' Britt answered, remembering a line about politics: you had to be comfortable drinking their booze and still not voting for them.

At the bar, a white-shirted attendant poured them champagne. At a few hundred a head, Britt wondered how much Veuve you would have to drink to get your money's worth.

She nodded at the security guard who had let her past with her wink and air of "don't you know who I am?" Poor Boris would have had to pretend to be a waiter.

Ant toasted her delicately. 'So, how do you support the party?'

'Anyway I can.' Britt smiled. 'But I am curious about Miles-Barclay. You were going to tell me about enemies?'

'Oh, nothing I know too much about. The people who hated him most were in his own party, which is always how it is.'

A round of applause and cheers went up as Kathryn Cambridge arrived with her husband and teenage daughter. Britt watched Ant, trying to get a reading, but his smile seemed genuine, as did most of the smiles around the room. Britt took this as further confirmation that one reason Australia was often governed by conservatives was that they hid their infighting better.

'So, most of the gossip about him was Greens focused?'

'Yes.' Ant took a sip. 'I believe for a single man he was,' he sniffed, 'popular.'

'With women?'

'I don't believe he was limited in that way. He was a Greens candidate after all.' His eyes lit up, clearly delighted with himself. Britt thought of the case and laughed along, promising to give money to Sea Shepherd as soon as she could.

'No long-term lovers?'

'I really wasn't that close to him. Different party, you know.' He shrugged. 'One thing, though. He seemed like the one person in the party who cared more for the people of Barwon than the oppressed millions overseas.'

'Oppressed millions?'

'You talk to most Greens people and you'd think we all had a personal debt to Palestine and Liberia. Try to raise something local, drug use for example, and they would spend half an hour of any meeting talking about climate change and influencing American foreign policy. Brandon didn't mind getting to the heart of it. He was even serious about the poaching issue.'

'Seahorses?'

His eye lit up, 'You've heard of it?'

'I did, yesterday. A local cop mentioned it.'

'I'm surprised. They don't seem too fussed either. Anyway, the Greens wouldn't touch it. I suspect because it was a cultural thing.'

'But it's nature.'

He sniffed without humour. 'You want to shut up a greenie, talk about indigenous hunting practices. Islanders killing sea turtles for food for example, it's hideous and torturous for the turtle, but our leftie mates won't say a word because that would be oppressing an oppressed people.' He drank, a bit fast. 'Yet, somehow, we're the racists.'

Britt had heard it before. Heaps of cops talked like this. She almost checked him for a gun. 'It's always hard when you're trying to find a goodie and a baddie.'

'Especially in this business. Miles-Barclay didn't mind grey areas. I suspect it's what made him so unpopular in some quarters.' He smiled. 'Enough about the Greens, how long are you down for?'

Andy burped. As the episodes wore on, he had enjoyed beer quickly then slowly. Embracing hedonism to spite his friends. He had even found some Cheezles in the pantry. They had gone well with the beer and made him forget that he hadn't had dinner. As he watched Buffy and company fight evil and occasionally each other, he couldn't help but imagine his own friendship group in such struggles, and kept glancing at the door to see if they were coming home. When they didn't walk through the door, he found himself looking north, not so much up the hallway as towards the street where Britt had indicated the dead politician had lived.

No. They weren't home, because they were daft. He wasn't daft, wasn't dead, and he was on holiday. He massaged the bridge of his nose and ate the last Cheezle, moving to swill it down with a beer that had somehow evaporated. He stood, a little unsteady, grateful there was no one to see it. Crossing to the fridge, he was greeted by cheese, eggs, mineral water and other things that weren't beer.

He rocked slowly against the door frame. He could hear a vampire singing about saving people and then killing them.

'Shit,' he said…

'I've found his laptop.'

'Surely it's locked.' Catherine said evenly.

Boris grunted as he typed a key. It asked for a PIN.

'What was his birthday?'

'11th of March,' Catherine answered immediately.

'Amazing. You just know this stuff.'

'Yes, I'm a savant like Sherlock Holmes. I also researched the details on the internet.'

'Once upon a time, you wouldn't have admitted that.' His fingers clicked over the keyboard.

'I still wouldn't if I needed to invoke mystique.'

Boris breathed out. 'It didn't work.'

'Worth a try.'

His year of birth didn't work either, neither did 6969, which Boris didn't tell Catherine he was trying. 'Should I take it?'

'What, with you?'

'Yeah, we could see if Neal can come down. He can do that kind of thing, can't he?'

Catherine was quiet a second. 'I'm sure he could get us in, but no. You're not a burglar. Hey, I can see your torch now. Turn a light on. I think it's less suspicious.'

'Five more minutes and I'm done.' Boris was aware of the sweat on his face, which was normal for the season, and his tee shirt, which usually would stay dry. He flicked a light on and surveyed the lounge room. 'Are you sure he was single?'

'Why? Bra? Tampons?'

'No, just, neat.'

Catherine snorted into his ear. 'Oh Christ, Boris. Some men grew up.'

'Hush.' Aside from some copies of *New Scientist* and yet another bookshelf, the lounge yielded nothing out of the ordinary. He looked at the pantry kitchen. It was so very ordered. Boris wasted twenty seconds confirming a hunch that Miles-Barclay's spice rack was indeed alphabetised. He blasphemed under his breath and surveyed the scene.

Almost nothing was out of place. There was an open packet of tea bags on the bench. Earl Grey, Boris noted, a detail that would almost certainly crack the case. Aside from that, a wooden chopping board was missing from a rack of three, a chopstick was slightly out of alignment in the cutlery drawer, and Miles-Barclay didn't appear to have either a cheese knife or side plates, anywhere.

Boris felt a small pain in his chest as he remembered not having them either until Molly had given some to him, just last month. Even a month ago, she was all in. You don't give side plates unless it's serious. What had gone so wrong so quickly?

'Ca-ar.' Catherine sing-songed over the line. Boris braced for it to rumble past.

'It's slowing.'

Boris heard it passing, oh so slowly. After the car seemed to have gone, he reached to switch the light off.

'Shit,' Catherine said. 'The car's coming back. Fast. Get out. Get out now.'

8

Generally speaking, people think about death while on holiday, because they're not thinking about holidays. Tragic, really.

~ Catherine Kint

Britt and Ant eased through the crowd to get outside, Ant begging to have a smoke. Britt didn't mind. She'd learned enough, but the drinks were free and he didn't seem too bad. He was thinning up top and had already mentioned being Prime Minister one day, but he was all right.

Beyond the door was a group of men definitely not in suits. They were more like bikies, and they all had the Australian flag on their denim jackets. Britt and Ant loitered on one side of the entrance. On the other, the probably-bikies kept to themselves, but were totally conspicuous among the short-hair, double-barrel-name crowd. 'Who're they?'

Ant was neutral. 'Local patriots.'

'As in?'

He cleared his throat. 'Patriots. Not everyone's friends in the party, but the local bikie chapter are pretty tame, and they command a real swathe of votes.' He sucked on his cigarette and spoke quietly. 'It's a broad church, our party, isn't it? Have you dealt with them?'

'Not these guys.'

Britt sipped her champagne and wondered what Boris was up to. Then one of the Patriots turned around and Britt had to breathe out slowly not to cough. There he was, outside and proud, and obviously with a political affiliation. Travis Barker.

She checked the others. Barker's rat-faced friend was definitely not one of them. The other two were big men as well; one bald and the other with a close crop up front and the tail of a mullet hanging across his collar. They drank beer from brown bottles and seemed relaxed.

'Do you enjoy dealing with them?' she asked Ant quietly.

'They have many views different to mine, but they love their country. I do too. I try to focus on where values overlap, not where they're different.'

'Hmm.' Britt said, suddenly sober. 'Please all, and you'll…'

'Please most, and usually stay in power,' he interjected, finishing his cigarette. 'Come on.' He opened his arm. 'I'll introduce you to Kathryn.'

From her perch near the bushy tree, Catherine watched, horrified, as the car roared back to the house, tyres screeching. It wasn't a cop car, but a red Holden. New model.

'Run.' She said quietly. Even though she could hear Boris's breathing was up.

'The bloody door is deadlocked. I'm going back out through a window.'

'Hurry, it's Duc.'

'Oh shit.'

Catherine felt a small stabbing pain in her guts. Nguyen was already at the fence.

Boris was well aware of a voice in his head telling him to breathe. He pushed his frame back through the window. He heard a rip and knew his shorts had torn at the crotch. His feet hit the ground and he pounded through the back yard, pushing shirts that were still on the washing line out of the way. As he got to the fence, he heard the yell. Duc was probably twenty metres behind him. Boris was over the palings before Duc's first syllable was complete. He stumbled, stood and lurched on through the nature clearing, pounding towards the pathway.

The trees were dense and large, mostly paperbark, with solid branches covered in a thick fuzz of small leaves. He did not want to be seen by Duc. On a whim, he diverted from the path and after a few metres he jumped the first two steps up a tree. He grabbed at branches to steady himself, already regretting the decision.

People panic upwards. The thought came to him unbidden, but he knew it was true. This was stupid. He wasn't running from a lion, but a cop. His instincts had failed him. His only hope was to get far enough up to be hidden. He stopped on a bough which bent, but didn't crack. He tried to calm his breathing. He heard the thump of Duc hitting the fence and the scrape of his boot against a paling.

Boris tried to move higher up, feeling the tiny leaves and twigs push into his back like small daggers. He could see the whole block through the leaves. Duc's face appeared over the fence, looking everywhere, then up the southern path as he heard a sound. Boris heard it too. A man. Singing. Badly. Then he saw a man stumbling up the path towards the clearing.

'Give me something to siiii–' The man promptly stopped, as he saw the dimly lit form of Duc coming over the fence. The man turned and ran. Boris wheezed in terror as Duc pounded through the nature reserve, tearing after the smaller man who disappeared down a laneway like a startled rabbit. Boris gritted his teeth as he heard the sound of the capture, a yelp and a pathetic, distinctly Celtic cry that could only come from one man that he knew.

Catherine could only stand and watch. Boris's connection had been lost. She was stuck in the rare position of not being able to think of a single way to help the situation. She had, in the forty-two seconds since Duc had run into the property, thought of slashing Duc's tyres – with a knife she did not have. Attempting seduction of Duc, which she felt would almost certainly be overplaying her hand. Or possibly trying to wrestle Boris free through physical prowess, and she didn't like her chances. She heard the cry of Boris being caught and swore in English, Cantonese, Greek and English again. She was trying to remember a rather colourful way of saying fellator of goats which she had been taught in Arabic when she heard what should have been Boris's voice and almost vomited in relief. Quickly she moved behind the bush, so she couldn't be seen, and also in case she did actually vomit.

'Ah come on. I've got nothing.' There was something in the pronunciation of "on" as a dipthong –"o-an" – that made her realise that Andy had come into the mix. 'There's no ransom, you bastard. I don't owe anyone cash.' He was being frog-marched to the red car, his arms pushed up behind his back by the bigger man. 'Police,' he shouted. 'Police.'

Houselights down the street came on. A man and woman came past with a golden retriever. 'Hey,' the woman called, her glasses flashing in the street light. She was late fifties and showed no fear as Duc pushed past. Her companion struggled with the dog lead.

'Help,' called Andy. 'This is a kidnap. I don't know this man. Call the police.'

Duc stopped shoving him. 'Oh, shut up. I am the police.' He kept Andy's arms pinned as he reached into his back pocket for his badge. Showing it to the woman, who seemed disappointed she couldn't make a citizen's arrest. 'Right,' the woman said. 'Okay then. Come on, Geoff.'

'Can I see that?' Andy's voice was high, and a little slurred. Duc held it in front of his face. Andy was quiet only for a second. 'What have you got on me then? I didn't kill the politician.'

'Oh sure.' Duc walked him to the red Holden. 'But why are you in his house, three days after he died?'

'I what?'

'You heard. Get in there. Watch your head.' He pushed Andy's head down and bundled him into the back seat of the car, then slid into the front seat and hit a button. Childproof locks, Catherine thought, and wondered how often his vehicle became a would-be divvy van.

'I wasn't in anyone's house. Hey, are you Duc?' Catherine thought she heard Duc swear as he drove off.

She exhaled. She was surprised at how much air she had been keeping in her lungs. She was reaching for her phone when she saw Boris emerge from the other side of the block. Catherine pointed down the street and they moved away on opposite sides of the road for a full eighty metres before they came together.

'What happened?' Catherine rubbed at Boris' hair, which seemed to contain a good deal more foliage than usual.

Boris' heart rate was obviously still up, even though his breathing had calmed down. 'You told me to get out. I ran. Pretty much stuffed the window. I got over the fence to that nature reserve and went up a tree.'

Catherine blew air. 'Great strategy.'

'Even by our standards.' He hiccupped and shook his head. 'So, I was basically just waiting to get caught and wondering if I want to do life in prison under a pseudonym or tell Britt I got caught and have her kill me.' A flash of moonlight washed over him and Catherine could see he was still sweating. 'And then Andy comes walking up the path singing to himself. Duc thinks he's me and takes him down and all I have to worry about is how to get down from the tree.'

'Timing.'

'I've never been so happy to see him.'

'He didn't even realise it was Duc. He thought he was being kidnapped.'

'How do we get him back?'

'Well, it wasn't a kidnapping but an arrest, so he's not in any immediate danger. I think we should tell Britt to pick him up.'

'Britt.' Boris said slowly.

'Yep. I think you should call Britt now and relay the situation.'

Boris took a few more steps as he considered this. 'Rock paper scissors?'

'Sure' said Catherine. 'But after a drink. Some news, no one can deliver sober...'

The candidate's face was quite close to hers, Britt thought. She had never been this close to a politician before, aside from when she had been part of a police guard for the Foreign Minister, back when she was a constable. At that time, all she had done was make eye contact, which breached protocol. She was sure the Minister's staff had registered it at the time, and was still waiting for the reprimand.

Where Kathryn Cambridge's staff were, hell knew. Cambridge's breath smelled slightly of grapes. 'Of course, it's a complete tragedy. I just can't help but think there may be a lesson in this.'

'Lesson?' Britt was only vaguely aware that her glass was empty. She was more interested in what lessons the possibly next Member for South Barwon could learn from the violent death of one of her rivals.

'It seems evident to me that Brandon was the victim of crime. Don't you think there's something in that? A representative from a party so hell-bent on being soft on crime is killed on the beach?' Cambridge spoke slowly, but Britt wondered how much wine she'd had. She quickly compared the woman in front of her with the wall posters. The living version was a little flushed.

'I think you could only say that about his ideology. Surely you don't mean he should be stabbed?'

'Oh God, no.' Cambridge checked her glass, which was almost empty.

'Did he have enemies, politically?'

'Not with us. Though, I wonder if you've heard?'

Britt leaned in, aware that a young man with short hair was approaching from the other side of the room.

Cambridge blinked as the music went momentarily down and the sound of Britt's phone was audible. Britt saw Catherine's name on her screen and paled.

'Excuse me.'

She moved over to a wall and held the phone to her ear. Britt could see own calm reflection in the glass windows as she asked a question, then one more.

As she heard the answer, Britt smacked her flat palm into the wall and let fly with a vitriolic description of how evolution had gone wrong to create such a friend as Catherine. It involved language not generally found in the Liberal Party charter.

Britt never felt nervous walking into a police station. It was familiar ground. She spoke the language and she knew where she stood. Tonight, walking into the Ocean Grove Police Station with a knot in her gut that wouldn't shift, wondering how she should approach this. She could play the hotshot detective pulling strings for a friend. That would work either quickest or not at all. Or should she be the respectful colleague mildly inconvenienced by a mix-up and nothing more?

If this went badly, she could be dismissed, or worse, if Thomas found out and asked questions. The weaselly bastard would almost certainly tell Williams, which would make life difficult.

There would be no formal counselling. No spats. Just word getting round that little Ms Houden wasn't always so clean. If she had testicles she could have five mistresses; but this was different. No rants about the patriarchy would change this situation. She was as sure of this as the knowledge that if she left this to Catherine and Boris, they might screw it up more.

Plus, Andy had sealed the deal by ringing her with his one phone call.

She imagined Williams in his grey suit, smiling his little smile and saying, as he often did, 'It's much easier not to have mates.'

She walked in. Took in the fluorescent lights and neutral colours. It looked like a typical police station. She quickly calculated how much wine she'd had and realised just as quickly that it was taking too long.

She decided to focus on the fact that she was Britt Damned Houden and she could do the job: Get the idiot out of the cells.

The sergeant who came out was the one who had been on duty the day the body washed in. 'Hello Madam. How can I help?' She'd nailed the requisite neutrality.

'My friend has been brought in. I think by mistake. His name is Andy McCafferty.' Britt was buoyed by the fact she hadn't slurred.

The woman's eyebrows raised. 'Ah, the Scotsman. He seems a little short for you.'

'Just a friend. De Carle.'

The woman regarded Britt sharply at hearing her own name. 'Who are you?'

Britt decided to play the Cop Card. 'Detective Britt Houden. Homicide. I was with you when Miles-Barclay washed up.'

De Carle nodded understanding. Almost genuflecting. 'Right.' De Carle opened the counter door. 'Come in. I didn't recognise you.' The lights flickered. Britt wondered if a curse was coming her way.

'Thanks. Is McCafferty okay?'

'Yes. I think it's a mix-up. An officer noticed a light on inside a murder victim's house and investigated.' Her voice dropped as Britt came to the cop side of the counter. 'The boss is pretty pissed off with the guy who brought him in. He wasn't on duty.'

'Right. He said something about a burglary?'

De Carle nodded.

Britt shook her head. 'The guy works at Melbourne zoo. He's not a burglar.'

De Carle grimaced. 'Yep, but he was pretty soused. We thought he should sleep it off even if he isn't a burglar. Come through.' The glazed door opened.

Four officers at desks didn't look up. Britt walked past an office and heard a familiar voice say quietly, 'It's just bloody scattergun, Luke. That woman on the CCTV needs following up.'

'You didn't like the surgical either, Selena.' Thomas' voice was louder, and Britt suddenly found something on the other wall extremely interesting.

She followed De Carle to the cells, checking for Duc and hoping she wouldn't see him until she had Andy out of sight. The force frowned upon off-duty arrests, but until now she'd thought it was a bit more lax in the country.

As they moved through a hallway, the sounds from the cells were the same as in any other station. A voice was singing *The Internationale* and another was whistling the chorus of *Always Look on the Bright Side of Life*. Britt instinctively moved towards the latter cell.

De Carle smiled wistfully at her. 'You really know your man, don't you?'

Britt returned the smile wanly and imagined, guiltily, and only for a second, Catherine's head smashing against the cell door, watermelon-like.

'I told you, he's not mine,' she answered. 'He's a free agent.'

'Not yet he's not. I could make him sweat if you want?'

'No, let him out.'

She had expected Andy to be desperate, but he was quite at ease. A sleepy eye winked at her.

'Are you here to rescue me? Good. Wait till I tell the Premier.'

Britt clenched her hands. 'On second thoughts, lock him up. Suddenly I'm sure he's committed several crimes. He mentioned something about drowning a Prime Minister.'

'Well, he's too young to have done Holt, so I think he's off the hook.'

Andy stood, briskly, barefoot and looking for his boots. 'Let's go. I've still got the diamond store to break into.'

Britt shivered in the heat. 'Shut up, Andy.'

'No, seriously. I want to make a complaint,' he said to De Carle.

Britt took hold of his upper arm.

'What's the complaint?' De Carle asked.

Andy looked at Britt, who towered over him. He pressed on. 'The soap in the cell wasn't organic. I don't know for sure, but a guy like me can tell.'

De Carle's face was impenetrable. 'I'll have it investigated.'

'Another thing,' Andy began.

Britt pulled on his arm. She almost felt Andy's bicep relocate.

'Nothing,' he said quickly. 'Lovely cell, great Feng Shui.'

Britt looked him over. Reedy, blinking and unsteady. Nothing screamed traumatised.

'Did they feed you?'

Andy shrugged. 'I wasn't going to be hung, no last meal. Quite famished now though.' He patted his small belly, then sat at a bench where his shoes were waiting. 'Where's that handsome fella? He was so sure I was a burglar.'

De Carle suppressed a grin at Nguyen's error. 'Everyone makes mistakes. Sorry about that.'

Britt was pretty sure that De Carle hated Duc, and that the dislike was mutual. De Carle was a stickler for rules and hierarchy, no doubt set to keep an eye on Duc's more watchman-like approach.

'No problem.' He bowed. 'Only Allah is perfect, eh?'

'If you would like to provide any more feedback, we have several forms online.'

Andy pulled his boots on. 'Sounds super fun. Any chance of a free set of handcuffs?'

Britt's mouth pursed. 'Let's go, Andy. Come on.'

'Sorry, Britt. I guess you work here.'

Britt looked towards the office, which was all clear for now. 'Not here, but, kinda.'

Andy took a last look at the cell. Britt imagined it was his first time in one. If he asked to take a selfie she would take De Carle's gun and end him. Instead, he walked out, pulling on his belt.

'You forgot to take this from me.'

De Carle smirked. 'Anyone as happy as you in the cells is hardly a risk.'

They walked back into the office and Britt moved quickly, head down, silently chanting a spell to not be seen.

'Houden.' Detective Luke Thomas' voice cut through the clicks of keyboards and the front desk phone ringing.

She turned. Thomas had set himself up in the sergeant's office. Sitting behind the desk, a facsimile of Williams', keyboard and photos sprawled across the desk. 'Hey, Thomas.'

'Nice dress.' He lifted his chin four degrees as he said it. Subtle he was not.

'Thanks. How's the case?'

'Oh.' He rolled his eyes. 'Up and down. Some people like doing things the hard way. Plus now I've gotta go to his house again.'

Britt didn't know where Perfetto was. Preparing some arsenic perhaps. 'Any leads?'

'Plenty. Twenty-two thousand people here in town. We've cleared four of them, including your mate there.' He pointed at Andy, with whom Britt refused to make eye contact. 'Talked to him about the break-in and just heard about how bad you are at volleyball.' He flashed a smile.

'Wanna get a drink later?' He picked up some papers as he said it, so she knew it wasn't important to him.

'Not tonight, Luke.'

His eyes flicked to Andy. 'Ah, I understand.'

Andy waved. 'Cheerio Detective, thanks for the wee chat, I can see why Britt talks about you so much.'

Britt again imagined Catherine's head splitting like a watermelon. She could practically hear it.

'What is the only Australian football team that is a palindrome?'

'Glenelg.'

'Christ, Boris, you didn't even think? I wasn't sure you even knew what a palindrome was.' Catherine was in her element: trivial pursuit, Boris and gin. A glass coffee table stood between them.

'I didn't, until I saw the same question on the telly about a decade ago. One question in a thousand sticks with you. It's what makes the game so good.'

'Challenging and occasionally attainable.'

'Have you ever played golf?'

'Twice.'

'You were terrible, right?'

'Boris.'

'Okay, you were you, but you weren't amazing. Come on. I'm building here.'

'Okay, I wasn't quite yellow jacket material. But I sank a twelve-foot putt.'

'Yes! That's it. That's the point.'

'Right. Challenging but attainable. You have glimpses of how brilliant you could become if you only devote your life to it.'

'Exactly.'

For the twelfth time in a half hour, both looked towards the door. Boris wasn't even hiding it anymore. Catherine, who was convinced they hadn't done anything wrong, was more circumspect. She was keen for the night to unfold. If there had to be a scene, so be it. They'd had them before.

Boris rolled the dice. A four. He moved the piece. He took a drink, then went back to watching the door. 'I really don't mind stepping on the cops toes, usually. Even hers. Tonight just had the extra element of feeling like I was wearing her shoes while I did it.'

'Your analogy is flawed at best, but as usual you're being very kind. She's a big girl, she'll be fine.'

The door swung open. Andy walked in holding a paper bag with a distinctly chippy smell. Britt came behind him, laughing at something he had said.

Andy ran through the room with his arms in the air. 'Yes. He is free. There is wind in his hair!' He spun, throwing the chips to Boris as he ran to Catherine's side 'Ethel, did you wait for me. Are you still... pure?'

Catherine gently smacked his face as Britt howled with laughter.

Catherine turned to her blonde friend. 'The gangs got to him in the big house, didn't they?'

'All messed up on goofballs,' Boris muttered, helping himself to a potato cake.

Britt walked to the fridge. 'Yep, he's a thug for life. Wanna beer, jailbird?'

'There's none left.' Andy countered.

'Hey!' Boris was wounded. 'I may not be the world's most successful burglar, but I know how to stock a fridge.'

Andy pumped his fist. 'In that case, I shall have the lager of freedom and it shall taste like the elixir of life.' He caught the can that was thrown to him.

Catherine shifted on the couch. 'What's going on, Britt? I was expecting fury from you and angst ridden noises from him. Is this a set-up?'

Britt cracked her beer and sat down heavily on the couch. 'Plausible deniability. I didn't know the house was getting broken into and between Andy's record and the fact that he seemed too drunk to scale a fence, they decided he could go.' She took a long sip. Cleansing, after taking an hour-long break from wine.

'Will Duc be for it?'

Britt pursed her mouth. The cheap beer was not as nice as the champagne at the Liberal Party shindig. 'From what I noticed at the station, I think they would all be screaming to get him transferred – he thinks too big for a small town.. Makes me like him even more. I'd tell him the truth, if it wouldn't put Boris in a cell.'

From the kitchen bench, where he was dutifully making Catherine a refill, Boris belched. 'Appreciated.'

'Some would be swayed by his good looks, Boris, but I'm a true friend.'

'Better keep an eye on Catherine then. She's mad for those high cheekbones.'

'I have many a reason to remain loyal to you, dear.' Catherine took the drink Boris passed her. 'Case in point,' she said, taking the glass. 'Plus, I'm no snitch.'

'Excuse me.' Andy's mouth was half full of chips. 'I was the one in the big house, and did I crack? I think not.'

Catherine stretched. 'Boris, would you give Andy a lap dance? I think it's tradition after doing time.'

Andy popped a chip. 'I'll pass this time. Keep your G-string where it is, big fella.'

Boris took a sip. 'Jail time has improved you. I haven't heard you complain in seven minutes.'

Andy grinned. Catherine had put some jazz on the stereo, and he nodded in time to it. 'For a second, I was scared because I thought I was going to die. Then I was scared because I thought I was going to prison. Then neither of those things happened. I called Britt; she came. I think, perhaps, I don't need to be as scared as I used to be. It's a nice feeling.'

Britt took charge. 'Pass the chips, Andy. Boris, tell me everything you found in Miles-Barclay's house. If we're going to prison, even for an hour, let's make it worth it.'

Boris took her through each room, Catherine reminding him of the details he missed.

Britt drained her can. 'You should have nicked the laptop.'

'I'm a burglar, not a thief.'

Britt shook her head. 'Yep. And I just don't know what Thomas is. I overheard him fighting with Perfetto, the word "scattergun" was used.'

Catherine was propped up on an elbow. 'How does he stay on in homicide?

Britt shrugged. 'He gets results.' She breathed out. 'So, between the drugs, the sex toys and the whispers at the political function, I'm feeling a bit like Thomas now. Twenty-two thousand in town, and I'm sure it wasn't four of them. Oh, I saw Barker there.'

Boris looked confused. 'At the station?'

'No, he was at the rally. Seems he's part of the local Patriots.'

Boris made a face. 'Skinheads?'

'They went out of vogue a decade ago; these guys are just as tough though.'

Catherine scrunched her nose. 'But now more politically active.'

'And connected,' Britt agreed.

'At a black tie event? Seems like a funny place for patriots.'

'It's a broad church in a surprising world.'

Catherine considered her chip. 'I thought nothing would surprise me anymore. Though, I was amazed you had your little black dress packed.'

'The modern woman is always prepared.'

'I brought mine too,' Andy countered. 'You bring yours, Boris?'

Boris called from the kitchen. 'I only brought my red one. What was I thinking?'

Catherine fetched a bottle of gin. This night wasn't done yet.

9

There should be a patron saint for all the funny, beautiful words lost to late nights and foggy memories. I would say a prayer to them often, if I remembered.

~ Catherine Kint

It was one of those slow mornings that should always happen on holidays. People drifted in and out of sleep, with no noise travelling through the house aside from breathing, the pad of footsteps and the muted happiness of a boiling kettle. When people did get up, there was an inclination toward couches, via the kitchen for hot and cold liquids rendered necessary by the indulgence of the previous night. By 9.30, they were all up, but three out of the four were still horizontal Boris, the lone man standing, was in the kitchen, and delicious smells filled the living room as he made breakfast without skimping on butter, salt or love.

Such was their synchronicity that hardly anyone spoke until they had all had three mouthfuls.

Andy put down his fork and said, 'I'm all in. I have to find out now.'

Catherine blinked in the sunlight streaming in the kitchen window. 'You're all in?' She shook the salt shaker with diminishing speed as his statement sunk in. 'Really?'

'Yep. If I'm doing time for it, I need to know.'

'Nice one,' Boris commented. Britt remained silent.

Catherine went straight into project management. 'Well, what do we know, and what do we need to know?'

Britt started. 'Andy, did Thomas give anything away when he spoke to you?'

'Only that's he's a dipshit and he thinks he knows what happened. He wasn't interested in me at all.'

Britt rolled her eyes. 'Okay. Miles-Barclay washed up with a stab wound that probably wouldn't have killed him.'

'He was fully clothed, but no report of him falling from a boat.'

Boris raised a hand. 'He had a healthy sex life.'

Catherine smiled gently. 'You don't know that, Boris. You're just assuming because you found weed, some vials and some handcuffs.'

Boris shrugged. 'It seemed a fair assumption. I thought it was wild.'

Andy cut toast. 'Maybe you should broaden your horizons.' Five seconds later, he became aware everyone was looking at him. 'What? You were all thinking it.'

Britt cleared her throat, avoiding Catherine's eyes. 'He wasn't universally liked in the Greens.'

Boris sipped coffee. 'I'm not sure anyone's universally liked by their own party, are they?'

Catherine shrugged. 'Maybe after you're dead, as in, long dead. And if you used to win a lot. I think they called it–' she made air quotes, '– brand connection.'

'As in, I agree with Lincoln about slavery and therefore I'm like Lincoln?' suggested Boris.

'Yep. I hate that I know that stuff.'

Andy put down his tea. 'I hate that now I know. I need a shower.'

Britt picked up her toast. 'It's a holiday. Nobody needs to shower.' She paused. 'Except Boris.'

Boris nodded. 'My best friends will tell me.'

Britt gave him a smile. 'These eggs are superb. Molly was a fool to leave you.'

The big man returned the grin. 'Agreed.' He nodded as if he was starting to believe it.

'We're getting off track,' said Catherine. 'What about the seahorse connection, Britt? Duc and your Liberal friend from last night indicated it was an issue that Miles-Barclay was open to looking at.'

Britt shrugged. 'Better that than more political rallies. I've been in more echo chambers this week than I need. I'll look up some good places to start. What else?'

Catherine chewed toast thoughtfully. 'I'm thinking of talking to Kayla's mum. If Barker killed Miles-Barclay, perhaps she's worried she's next?'

'I thought they were separated?' said Boris.

'I think they are,' replied Britt, 'and there's a stepdad, but it's a small town. Sadly, being separated doesn't keep you any safer from violence than being together.'

Boris took out his phone. Catherine's eyes lit up. 'Did you take the photo of those vials last night?'

'Shit. I was going to, but there was no memory left on the phone. I need to delete some pictures.' He turned the screen around. 'I really don't need all these photos of Molly playing with cats.'

Britt was deadpan. 'No, you really don't.'

'I wonder if it was...' Boris' fingers tapped on the phone. 'No.'

'What? Did you remember a seahorse clue?'

'For a second, I did, but now I can tell you that it's not called "Mah Jong."'

As Catherine rolled her eyes, Britt looked up from her own phone. 'Dried seahorse is used in Chinese medicine, remember? Did the symbol on the vials look like this?' she spun the phone around, showing the Cantonese writing to Boris.

He stared at it for ten seconds. 'I'll say yes.'

Britt held out her hand. 'Yes, they did?'

Boris handed the phone back. 'Yes. They were probably the same language as that.'

Catherine sighed deeply. 'That was a long shot anyway.'

Britt was back on her phone. 'There's a marine sanctuary on the other side of the bay. We could head over on the ferry and see what we can find out.'

Catherine sipped her coffee. 'It seems a long way to go for background on something that could be completely unrelated.'

'You're right,' Britt said. 'We should all stay with you and hassle Kayla's mum.'

Catherine puffed her cheeks out. 'Okay, good point. If we don't have many leads we should at least do something fun.'

'If we're so short on leads, why was that car following us?'

'Because you're beautiful, Detective. I would follow you home too.'

'You're having so much fun with this, aren't you?'

As Catherine smiled like the proverbial cat, Andy stretched his arms, post-meal. 'I quite fancy the ferry. Last time I was on it there were dolphins.' He stood, picking up keys. 'I think I left my hat in your car, Britt.'

'I'm in,' said Boris. 'Unless you need backup, Catherine?'

'No. I'll go solo today. My gut tells me it's a good day for lone wolf.' She started clearing plates. 'It's a safe town. Did you notice no one even stalked us last night?'

'You're right,' said Boris. 'One of us just got arrested.'

They heard the yelp from downstairs.

Either Andy had hit his head on the car, or something was wrong.

Forty seconds later, Britt looked again at the stab wound in the back-right tyre of her green station wagon, a small screwdriver still in the gash. The car stood at a forlorn angle as if it could sense the detective's mood.

'Now that's rude.' Britt slammed her palm on the boot of her car. 'Stalking is one thing, but this is just inconvenient. I'm on holiday, for Christ's sake.'

Catherine came out with a plastic bag. 'Want to take it for prints?'

Britt took the bag. 'I'm sure the local cops will say it's kids, and going to them might risk talking to Thomas.' She looked at the screwdriver. 'The twit would see this as a case breaking clue then rough up a minority. I think if we're spending the day on a murder, we just widen the focus and find the arsehole who did this as well.'

'And take him in?' Boris asked, pausing in his search of the small front garden. Britt cracked a knuckle. 'And murder him too.'

'Don't worry.' Catherine patted Britt's back. 'Boris is great at changing tyres.'

Twenty-five minutes later, Catherine was walking alone into Ocean Grove. Now it was the weekend the town was fuller than usual. She passed a bakery on the main drag and had the strange sensation of not wanting anything, even though she was on holiday. She didn't even crave coffee. For a second she stood and simply absorbed the warm air and loud colours.

There was no work, there was a mystery, she was alive, and Boris was probably swearing as he changed a tyre that Britt was certainly capable of changing herself. A most satisfactory moment on earth. She gave both the creator and chaos a spiritual high five.

Catherine started at the supermarket where she'd last seen Kayla, and the girl had indicated her mother was inside. It was difficult to know who to look for, as she didn't know what Kayla's mum looked like. Andy had suggested checking on social media, but Catherine felt a) it was creepy to cyberstalk someone you didn't want to be friends with, even for a good cause and b) it would involve the kind of smartphone and armchair investigation she avoided.

The supermarket was heaving with people. The shelves were somehow still full to burst with white rolls, roast chickens and savoury biscuits. Catherine picked a middle-aged staff member at random. 'Hi.'

Half-moons of flesh dangled under a pair of the tiredest eyes Catherine had ever seen. The woman had a halo of dyed white hair, and from the depths of her soul, she forced a smile. 'Ya?'

'My friend Kayla said her mum works here.'

'And?' Catherine wondered if she was about to say 'Aisle eight' out of habit. Then she spoke again. 'What's her name, Kayla's Mum?' Her accent sounded Spanish.

'I'm not sure. Kayla's a new friend, but she asked me to pass on a message.' Catherine squinted in the crushingly bright light of the supermarket. She turned as the woman looked past her. 'Dot,' she half yelled. 'What's Janine's daughter's name? Is it Kayla?'

'Nah.' Called Dot, who Catherine couldn't even see for the bulk of shoppers. 'Her daughters are Sharnie and Angelique.'

The white halo shrugged at Catherine. 'Sorry. Can't help you.'

Dot's voice came again from either in the Far East or the cereal aisle. 'Raylene's got a Kayla.'

'All right. Thanks, Dot.' Halo-head looked back at Catherine. 'Out the back. I think she's getting trolleys in.'

Catherine walked out, never wanting to set foot in a supermarket or possibly a city ever again. There was something about the brightness, the music, the way that her happiness had dissolved near the deli that made Catherine decide that evolution had gone extremely wrong and she would welcome the next sabretooth tiger that ripped her limb from limb.

A shopping trolley conga was moving like a steel Chinese dragon through the car park at the rear. The woman pushing it was small and wiry and her stance told Catherine she had a rolled cigarette in her mouth.

She herded the trollies with a boxer's tenacity. She had a fierceness to her, her movements were sharp and economical.

'Trolleys are round front,' she called by way of greeting. Catherine was sure it was the same voice that had called Kayla's name three nights earlier, on the day that Miles-Barclay's body had washed up.

'I don't want a trolley, Raylene.'

The older woman's face hardened. Her short hair seemed like an extension of the lines that flowed around her eyes. 'You are?'

'I'm Catherine. I've spoken to Kayla a few times. She's worried about you.'

'Fuck off, cop. I'm not talking.' Smoke spilled from her mouth as she started pushing the trolleys.

'I'm not a cop. I make hats.'

'I'm still not talking.' She sounded just like Barker. Her head flicked three ways quickly. She went back to pushing. Catherine got in her way.

'I hear you've been worried. Maybe I can help.'

Raylene exhaled smoke and threw her cigarette away. 'So, you're the nosey bitch?' Her eyes flicked again. 'Someone said you were pretty.'

Plenty of people were around, but no one was paying them any attention. Their voices were low.

'Are you worried about someone watching you, Raylene?'

'I'm working. You're in my way. I don't care who you are. Get out of the way.' She pushed hard at the trolleys. Catherine jumped on board for a second and smiled as she rolled, but Raylene thrashed the line of trolleys and Catherine had to jump off.

'Stay out of our work,' Raylene muttered as she pushed the steel dragon back to the market.

'Or you'll what? Stab our tyres with a screwdriver? Park outside our house while we sleep?'

The trolley's stopped with the rattle of a train. Raylene regarded Catherine with still, cold eyes.

'Not me, bitch.' She said quietly. 'Wrong again.'

As it happened, Boris and Britt had changed the tyre together, while Andy made another cuppa for all three of them. So, it was a happy group that set off for the Buckley's Marine Reserve, thirty-five minutes behind the previously agreed schedule. Boris took the front seat because Andy wanted to read an article about seahorse poaching on his phone.

Britt took the wheel and decided not to change the radio station from classic hits.

'So, what's your thought?' Boris was staring at the sky as he spoke. Britt knew he would sneeze in the next twelve seconds.

'Enjoy the ferry, find the clue and catch the killer?'

'You left out lunch,' Andy called from the back seat.

'Yes, and lunch. Scotty hasn't had a fish supper in almoost twealve hooers.'

'I sound nothing like that,' Andy chided. 'Just becorse a fellah loykes cheeps when hees on holidaiy.'

Britt snorted. 'And I sound nothing like that. You just added a bunch of Rs and Os to your own accent.'

'Yeah well, pretend I was naming my unborn children in the Australian tradition.'

Britt rolled her eyes and decided to answer Boris.

'What do you mean, what's my thought?'

Boris let fly with a thunderous sneeze.

'Bless you,' Andy said disinterestedly, not looking up from his phone.

'Thanks,' Boris sniffed. 'By "what's your thought" I mean, who do you think stabbed your car?'

'Oh right.' Britt drove for fourteen seconds as she thought about it. 'I don't know.'

'It's cool that you thought about it.'

'You?'

'I suspect it's a civilian, as the Police just lock us up when they catch us. It could be the killer. Maybe that Kayla girl.'

'They stabbed the car about as effectively as Miles-Barclay was stabbed.'

'That's bothering you, isn't it?'

Britt's face was impassive as she pulled into traffic. 'Yep. I want to know the autopsy findings. I'm ninety per cent sure that the wound wouldn't have been fatal.'

'How do you know that?'

'I know how a fatal one looks.'

'Good point. I shall suggest you're a subject matter expert on stabbing from now on.'

'Subject matter expert?'

'I saw it on telly.'

She changed gears. 'Should have guessed. What's bothering me is what makes a stabbed person go, or stay, in the water?'

Andy's head came forward. 'Surely it was stay? You wouldn't run into the water after that.'

'So how did he get stabbed in the surf?' Boris asked.

'Maybe he wasn't,' suggested Andy.

Boris frowned. 'What do you mean?'

'Well Britt here says it wasn't a clean stab wound. Maybe he was swimming and fell or a wave dumped him on to something sharp? It could be there was no crime and we could be sunning ourselves now and discussing cocktails.'

Britt winced. 'You're not talking drinks already? I'm still feeling like I drank cement.'

'Well no,' Andy conceded. 'But I do wonder if there was no stabbing at all.'

Boris sniffed, staring at an ad for a minigolf course. 'That theory falls over when we get back to question one.'

'Eh, remind me?'

'Who stabbed my car?' obliged Britt.

'Maybe that guy.' Andy pointed to the right. Britt saw what he saw and slowed the car.

Travis Barker was on Tuckfield Street; a side street off the main road out of town. He had in his hands the lapels of another large man. All things considered, it was a poor place to be visibly violent when you were a suspect in a murder and should be keeping a low profile. The large man's glasses were skewed and his curly hair wild as he tried to get away.

Only then did Boris realise how big Barker was. He'd only seen a photo previously. Barker must have been at least six three and brawny. He had a look to him that Boris couldn't place, but suspected it came from long years locked up with other violent men. He had a readiness to violence equivalent to Boris' readiness to laugh.

Boris was glad when Britt took charge.

'Oi.'

Barker and the man both turned to them; Britt was already out of the car and walking towards them. Boris was amazed at the zero hesitation she showed as he scrambled to follow. The large man's feet hit the ground as Britt approached.

'Is everything all right?' Britt's voice was cop perfect. The heavily unsaid 'or do I need to make it all right?' lingered in the air. Barker's eyes went blank, though his jaw remained tense.

'No issue here.'

'Who are you?' the large man called.

Barker hissed something at him. Britt ignored it. The large man's eyes widened, and then again when Boris and Andy got out of the car.

'I'm a concerned citizen, that's all,' continued Britt.

'No issue here, citizen.' Barker's tone was neutral even as his voice was deep. Britt had a flash, seeing him in his Patriots gear the night before.

'What about you?' She looked at the large man.

He was staring at their car. Britt suspected he would have blown over the limit had she been doing breath tests.

'Sir?' she called again.

'Golledge.' Barker's voice snapped him out of it.

'No issue,' Golledge said quickly. He blinked at her a few times. Shook his head. Britt began considering if he were mentally ill rather than intoxicated. 'I was just talking. I'm going now.'

He started in the direction of town.

Britt paid close attention to Barker's body language. His chin was up, and the tension remained in his jaw. The man's beard did nothing to hide it. He watched Golledge walking away then checked Britt, who hadn't moved. Barker looked at her like she was a cop, which in his estimation made her lower than pond scum, then walked the other way. He shook his head slightly as he did.

'Patriots thing?' Boris watched Barker's retreating form.

Britt shook her head. 'Big bloke didn't seem the type.' She tapped the wheel. 'Golledge. That's Catherine's weird friend.'

Andy put a hand on the car door. 'Robbery?'

Britt got back in the car. 'Not Barker's MO.'

'Didn't he do time for robbery?'

Britt released the handbrake. 'Aggravated burglary.'

'What's the difference?'

'One can mean lots of things, from pickpocketing to art theft. Agg burg is strictly being in someone's space and hurting someone in the process, usually the owner.'

Barker walked away.

'They don't come much tougher,' observed Boris.

'He's got this mate with a rat's tail,' Britt said. 'He strikes me as the really dangerous one.'

Boris sniffed. 'I'll be sure to avoid him then.'

Catherine perambulated back up the Terrace while she thought about the previous interaction. Two things that stuck with her. Raylene was not scared of her, but was definitely scared of something. She also knew that Catherine had been asking around, just as Kayla had.

Catherine gave a minute's pause to think about her possible admirers or haters. As she didn't know who they were, she would call them admirers. She then decided that even hatred was some twisted form of admiration. The whole idea put a spring in her step.

A timely spring, as across the street was Duc Nguyen in uniform. His uniform looked great, though the long pants in the heat of the day seemed cruel... He was patrolling solo and had spotted her too. He waved, but gestured ahead and kept walking. Catherine followed where he was pointing, deciding she could find room in her schedule for that too, whatever it was.

In two blocks, his destination became apparent.

Catherine sighed as she found herself at yet another political rally. The green shirts formed a mob and then became a wave.

Catherine pushed her way into the crowd as a bespectacled man in a white shirt, one of the Green's more prominent federal senators, gave a rousing speech about integrity and vision before introducing Shelby Acland, the new candidate for South Barwon. He hugged her and led her onto the small dais.

Shelby took the microphone, smiling warmly at the senator. She scanned the crowd and started.

'I am honoured to be named as Brandon's successor. He and I worked together on this fight, and that I am standing here is a symbol. A symbol that our fight cannot be stopped, and we cannot be stopped. In the days since his death, we have seen a lull in the attacks on our party, but they will come again. These attacks always come from the same quarters, those on the wrong side of history. Those who, even in this beautiful place, cannot see what damage we are doing to the planet. I will continue our fight as we come together in unity.'

There was a slight delay on her vocals, so the last syllable of "unity" echoed across the crowd.

Catherine's eyes fell on the person she was looking for. Yvonne McSweeney was blank and attentive. Catherine watched her as Shelby spoke again.

'Now is the time for environment, education, health and indigenous rights to be our unified message to the political discussion.'

Yvonne's mouth flickered a couple of times at that sentence, but her control was excellent. She must have known people were watching her. Catherine wondered how the preselection fight had been conducted.

'This is a time for our voices to grow louder, to swell in the memory of Brandon. Now is the time for change in the narrative of our land and it will come through our collective voices. I am standing in Brandon's place, but just as I do that, any of us could stand here and deliver the same strong message. I will represent South Barwon. I will represent our party and I will represent Australia's future. A strong future. A Green future. Our future.'

Strong cheers met the announcement. Shelby stepped down in front of news cameras and radio microphones as hip-hop beats issued from the speakers.

Catherine made her way through the throng, recognising at least three people from Brunswick. She found Yvonne briefing three green-clad staffers.

'You stay in town. You go with Shelby to Geelong and you take the Senator to Torquay for the 1pm rally. Ignore any redshirt trouble, but get it on camera if they go too far.' The listeners all voiced assent and moved on.

'Three references to unity in a one-hundred-word speech. Was that a message to the party or you?' Catherine made sure her voice was light.

Yvonne smiled. 'I'm a happy little Vegemite as Volunteers Manager.'

'I've heard that line before. Although, you do look like you're in your element.'

Yvonne was looking past her, tapping her own clipboard with a pen. 'If you want fast-paced, do a campaign. If you win a campaign, you can do fast-paced for years.' A shadow crossed her face. 'It also distracts me from Brandon.'

The crow's feet around Yvonne's eyes darkened as she said his name. 'You were close.'

Yvonne nodded. 'So I keep it fast-paced, by choice, not just tradition.'

'Grief aside, is it the best way to get things done?'

'No one has time to be thinking about that.'

Yvonne started walking. Catherine fell into step. 'Any word on the investigation?'

'A little.' Yvonne's mouth pursed slightly. 'It seemed contradictory. Police are moving towards a conclusion but are interested in a woman seen on CCTV footage. Apparently, it will hit state television this afternoon. That's all war room chatter by the way.'

'I'd like to know more. Buy you a beer?'

'Still a cop, huh?'

'Just curious.'

Yvonne checked her watch. 'We're done here in half an hour and before I leave for St Leonards, I have twenty minutes to kill. At which point, yes, you can buy me a beer. Zebra bar, know it?'

Catherine nodded. 'Half an hour. Thanks for the trust.'

'You'd have found out anyway. Vote for us.'

Catherine winced. 'I'm from Brunswick.'

Yvonne was herding green-shirted people towards the cameras, but briefly caught Catherine's eye. 'Of course you are.'

10

On any given day, I see the future as either slavery or utopia. I can see both with equal clarity. It's why I fight so hard.

~ Yvonne McSweeney

'Isn't that beautiful?' Britt pulled up at the marine reserve car park.
'Worth the trip, even if we get nothing,' Boris agreed.

The expanse of beach in front of them was panoramic and ideal. Long swathes of sandy shore were met by staggered natural jetties of rock, with pools glistening in the late morning sun. The tide was out, with small waves lapping low at the shoreline. Between the carpark and the beach was a garden lush even in the summer. Families were picnicking, and gulls sailed through the air above them.

'Now see this? You really don't get this in Fife.' Andy donned his sunglasses as he stepped out of the car. 'If you just made everything grey and everyone more miserable, you'd be a lot closer.'

'Yeah, but so much of Scotland is beautiful,' said Boris. 'Do you remember the train trip the other day?'

'To Geelong? Yeah, I do.'

'Hardly a trip through the highlands.'

'Aye,' he gestured dismissively. 'But this'll do.'

They walked through the park. Britt touched the leaves of trees lightly as she passed.

'You're softening on this holiday,' Boris teased.

'Just smelling the damned roses,' she said in mock reproach. 'People

104

never get murdered in places like this; or when they do I'm too busy to notice the beauty.'

'So, we're just here trying to solve a murder.'

Britt's voice was breezy. 'I'm not being paid, and no one is crying on me. I can see why you have more fun than me, usually.'

'I like it when I'm pouring pints and Catherine's whinging about fashion shows.'

The path took them to a small round building of wood and concrete, dominated by long blue windows.

'Let's split up,' Britt told them. 'You two go and find out what you can about seahorses. I'll play the cop card on the front-of-house staff.'

'Should you go in first?' asked Boris.

'Yep. You two look like blokes on holiday.'

'You look like a woman on holiday.'

Britt straightened. 'Not when I walk like this, I don't.' She strode through the doors exuding more authority than a high court judge.

Boris turned to Andy. 'You reckon they get taught how to do that?'

'Act urgent and impatient? Mate, it's not just cops. Half the people I know do that, especially at the zoo. I think I slept through that class.'

'You and me both.'

Britt was amazed by the calmness inside the building. The windows, tinted a light blue, seemed to be a natural sedative for the people inside. At least fifteen people were in the space, all looking at exhibitions and reading plaques, including a half dozen children. They were so quiet Britt thought she had transported into a new, polite dimension. She had been in rowdier libraries.

A large, bald man with a beard greeted her at the front counter. His Italian accent was confirmed by his name badge – Giuseppe.

'Hello. I'm Britt Houden from the homicide squad.' Her finger twitched as she almost reached for a badge that wasn't with her. 'I need to talk to someone about seahorse poaching.'

'Of course.' He picked up a phone and dialled. 'Bella, there's a police officer here. Can you come out?' He looked at Britt. 'Do you have a warrant?'

Britt shook her head. Giuseppe said into the phone, 'No, no warrant. Okay, thank you.'

He hung up. 'Bella will be just a minute.' He gestured towards a wall, as if there were a couch to sit on.

A black door that Britt had assumed was a fire escape opened a second later. A woman in a pale blue uniform shirt appeared and made a beeline for Britt. She had large eyes and a face that looked like it smiled easily.

'I'm Bella Cunningham, Assistant Director here. Can I help you, officer?'

'I'm a detective with homicide, but call me Britt. I'm actually off duty. I need some information on seahorse poaching in Port Phillip Bay. Particularly on the eastern side.'

Bella gave a slow blink. 'I'd be happy to talk sometime, Detective, but not at short notice. You could make an appointment with Giuseppe here–'

'It won't take long. I'm just after some background. I need some expert advice.' She brought her chin down an inch. 'A man has died. Can you help?'

Bella waited a beat. She brought out her phone and checked the screen. 'My next meeting's in fourteen minutes. Why don't you come through to the office?'

'Perfect. Thanks.' Britt followed her through the black door.

Bella's office was small, but one-way windows made up two of the walls, giving privacy as well as a view of the beach and the gardens. The other walls were covered in shelving on which stood several rows of white file holders. There was also a small painting of a grey seagull against a night sky, which Britt thought, given the spectacular views of the office, was one of the least needed pieces of bad art anywhere. Perhaps it was standard issue in the public service.

'I don't usually deal with issues around poaching. Isn't that a Federal Police matter?' Bella sat behind her desk at an ergonomic seat with no back. She gestured to Britt towards one of the chairs opposite.

'Usually yes, but in this instance, we believe that it may be connected with another crime.' Britt didn't mention murder. Sometimes, to be effective in an investigation, you had to keep it dry. She'd already mentioned someone was dead.

'So, what do you need to know?'

'Well, until a couple of days ago, I wasn't sure there were any seahorses in Port Phillip Bay. Am I right in thinking there is enough to stock a trade for poachers?'

Bella nodded. 'There are syngnathids in all parts of the bay, and all around the Victorian coast. In the bay, there's dozens of different species, primarily pot bellies and the short head seahorse. I believe most of the poaching, though, is for the weedy sea dragon, which is stolen for aquariums and largely exported.'

Britt's eyebrow rose. 'I was told that seahorse poaching is more for Chinese medicine.'

Bella typed into her keyboard. 'To the best of my knowledge, a dried seahorse is worth about $40, a weedy sea dragon alive will get you about $100. I suspect your average poacher will diversify.' She read off her screen. 'Of the forty arrests for poaching syngnathids last year, twenty-two involved sea dragons.'

Britt confirmed her suspicion that syngnathids meant seahorses and stuck to the questions she had prepared. 'Good point. Is there any legal harvesting?'

'Collection permits are possible, but not for commercial purposes. The animals are protected so it's extremely rare. Generally speaking, if people have seahorses, it's outside the law.'

'Where would you collect them from? Within five k's of shore?'

'More like within 100 metres. They live in reefs and seagrass meadows.' She turned the screen around, showing underwater plant life that resembled something from an oceanic episode of *The Muppets*. 'Generally, at a depth of 15 metres, 30 at the most. You could find them snorkelling, though I imagine a poacher would have some scuba gear.'

Britt took a note. 'What time would you get them?'

'They're diurnal.' She saw Britt's frown. 'I mean they're more active in the daylight, but I believe the best time to hunt would be early in the morning or late at night. That's more for avoiding police than anything else.'

'How big is the problem?'

Bella blew air out her nose. 'I'd say not as big as climate change or drug running, but there's money in it and demand. For a small group of people, it's their bread and butter.'

'What would you use to get them?'

'Standard poaching stuff really. Nets, snorkel. A dinghy? A boat? The scientists we deal with use cameras but we're more about recording and preserving.'

'Powder is a form of preservation,' Britt observed.

'Not great for repopulation though. My meeting is coming up. Any other questions?'

Britt checked her notepad. 'Have you heard of a group running poaching rings?'

Bella's forehead creased. 'Usually, it's lone wolves on this side of the bay. I did hear about a group that was working on the west side about a year ago. Near Queenscliff.'

'What are they called?'

Bella looked blank. 'Poachers. They don't have a gang name or anything.'

'Oh, right.' Britt cleared her throat. 'Thanks. Enjoy your meeting.'

Bella put on a headset. 'I probably won't, but I have a great view.'

Britt emerged to find the display area still as full and inexplicably quiet as when she left. She sniffed the air for sedative in the air conditioning. Nothing. Perhaps it was being so close to the beach but with the feeling of a research station. According to Catherine's regular rant, humans craved belonging and significance. Britt thought that working here, the sea would give belonging, and the research, significance. For a second, she considered a career change.

No – too many bad guys to catch.

She found Boris and Andy staring at different displays. Boris was hunched down to read a plaque clearly meant for children. Andy standing five metres away, also reading. He called to Boris as she approached.

'Hey, was this the word?'

Andy was pointing at a photo of two yellow seahorses that Britt assumed were pregnant until she saw the name – the Pot-Bellied Seahorse. It explained the disproportionate white guts of the two. Andy was indicating the part of the display on poaching. Boris examined the Cantonese symbols.

'Yep, I'm pretty sure that was it.'

'Hai Ma,' Andy read the English translation.

'I was never going to remember that.'

Britt joined them. 'True, but you didn't help by continually repeating the words "Mah Jong" every time we asked you.'

'I had one word right.'

Andy said to Britt, 'Did you find anything?'

'I got some good background. Let's go.'

Andy was crestfallen. 'We've only been here twenty minutes.'

Britt checked her watch. It was early. 'Fine. I'll go back to the bakery down the road. You guys get us a picnic table and I'll brief you over a pie. Okay?'

Andy raised his joined hands in triumph. 'Business *and* pleasure.' As Britt walked away, he nudged Boris. 'I'm gonna get that tattooed in Hindi.'

Boris looked skywards. 'Whatever you think will help, Scotty.'

Catherine put the drinks on the table. As far as she was concerned, this day was going brilliantly. 'Are you holding up okay?'

Yvonne eyes flashed dark and she shook her head. 'I'm too busy to think of it.' She stared at the pint in her hand as if it held the secrets of the universe. 'I'm told that the party has over 10,000 new members state-wide in the past two days. It might not seem like a good price for a death, but I know Brandon would be happy with it.' She puffed her cheeks. 'Even winning the Lodge wouldn't be enough for me.'

'For your death?'

'For Brandon's.'

They clinked glasses. Yvonne took a slow and considered pull.

'A special guy,' said Catherine.

'Yes, but people always say that about people after they've died. I said it about Brandon when he was alive, even when he was a rival. He was one of those people who could keep a party together, just because you knew if you were on his side, you were on the right side.'

'He was a true believer.'

Yvonne took another sip. 'Someone has to be.'

'Getting cynical?'

'I've been in politics for a decade. You think I'm only getting cynical now?'

Catherine smiled, giving Yvonne the point. 'How was Brandon's love life?'

Yvonne sipped again. 'Interesting, I believe. He was single, but had had a few major relationships. He was even with Shelby for a year. His political life was more turbulent.'

'Wait, you mean Shelby, the current candidate?'

'Yep. We're not putting that in the papers. It's a poor narrative and Shelby's partnered to some lawyer in Sydney who only turns up at campaign launches. Also, things were rocky between her and Brandon in the past few months.'

Catherine rubbed the condensation on her glass. 'Was he still in love with her?'

'God, no. He was more focused on getting preselected by the party. They were rivals in that. It got a little ugly.'

'How so?'

Yvonne looked hard at Catherine, weighing up what she could say. 'They had equal numbers. It was coming time for the party to meet when some claims of bullying from Shelby's past were leaked to the local press.'

'Shelby was complained about?'

Yvonne nodded, her tight curls echoing to her movements. 'By a couple of temps at Shelby's day job, Legal Aid. Their HR investigated. She was found to have done nothing wrong, but bullying is a buzzword in the Greens, and it swung support to Brandon.'

'Did he leak it?'

'He said he didn't, but if I'd been him I would have done it.'

'Shelby took it badly?'

'Not so badly as to kill him. If that's what you mean.'

'I hadn't quite got there.' Catherine shifted. 'I was just intrigued.'

Yvonne exhaled slowly. 'I know how it feels to not get preselected. But Shelby wants it more than anyone I've ever met. I've seen her house. She hoards mementos of her life. Her acceptance letter from the Party. A note from the leader. Even a cup that she made a coffee for the Prime Minister with.' Yvonne rolled her eyes. 'All leading to the point where she prevails. She really has a sense of destiny.'

Catherine hummed. It sounded like a schoolmate of hers. She pushed the thought away. 'The leak. Would you really have done it?'

'Well, no. But if I were him and I didn't have my morals.' She finished her pint. 'They're a terrible curse, but I sleep well. See you round, Catherine.' As she stood up, her mobile beeped. She checked as she was leaving, then stopped and sighed. 'The candidate has been held up by a national interview for the telly. She postponed the St Leonards event by half an hour.'

Catherine's own drink had also evaporated. 'Let me fill in your time.'

Yvonne put down her bag as Catherine ordered at the bar. It was early, and the only other customers were a couple sitting on the balcony, in silence, staring at the main street. Her head was on his shoulders; he stroked her hair. The woman's hair was a similar colour as her own, but with a single grey streak. Catherine thought of Duc and aging, briefly, like a name whispered in a dream before you wake.

'Here you go, love.' The publican's voice was rougher than sandpaper, but she smiled every time Catherine came to the bar.

Yvonne was texting when Catherine got back to the table. She looked up gratefully as Catherine placed the pint in front of her.

'Thanks.' She went back to her phone. 'It speaks bloody volumes. She took the national interview over the rally for people who might actually vote for her. She doesn't care about this place.'

Catherine sipped her gin. 'A lot of people in South Barwon watch national television.'

'Yeah, that's what the coms people are saying, but they're from the Federal Party, so it works for them. Give me a sec.' Her thumbs went double time. 'I've got to email the volunteers.'

'It's a strange seat. You've got hippies, libs, workers. My friend even saw Patriots last night.'

Yvonne put her phone down. 'Yeah, did you hear about Brandon and the Patriots?'

Catherine leaned in. 'No.'

'They hated him. Even before he was the candidate. He humiliated them.'

'How?'

'They were having one of their rallies in the outskirts of Melbourne. Doing their usual fearmongering and wishing that Bob Menzies would come back from the dead and ride shotgun for Jesus. We did an anti-racism rally down the road, in a park. Heaps of cops around, keeping us apart, but I think most of us liked that. Those Patriots are scary dudes. Brandon was making a speech, pretty much the same as everyone else's, about not fearing and open hearts. Then he got this look and said, "I don't know why I'm talking to the people who agree with me". Then he gets off the stage and walks to the Patriots rally. Alone. Someone tried to go with him, but he waved them off. We followed, but the cops stopped the main group. Brandon walked to the edge of the Patriots group and started speaking to them, first to those at the outskirts, then as more and more people realised he was a lefty they formed this circle around him. They started their chanting about halal and sharia law. Brandon just kept talking. He wouldn't stop. Then one of the Patriots walks out to him and gets in his face. The bloke is huge. Brandon was only five foot seven. Their crowd is cheering, while ours is horrified and starts screaming at the cops.'

Yvonne's voice went lower, a natural storyteller. 'Brandon doesn't stop talking. He's not yelling, he's not crying. In fact, he's smiling. He's got a man a head taller than him yelling bile into his face and Brandon is smiling. He wouldn't stop talking. He keeps saying "there is nothing to fear". Really calmly.

'The big bloke starts to get frustrated, calling his comrades over, but they don't budge. He turns back to Brandon and smacks him a backhander. The cops charge in, and that was the photo in the papers. A big thug hitting a smiling lefty. It made Brandon a star in the party.'

'He was all right?'

'Lost a tooth, but fine. He talked about it at some rallies. He knew the guy who hit him. He was a local bloke. He'd just come out of prison.'

Catherine took a punt. 'Travis Barker, perhaps?'

'That's him.' Her mouth twitched. 'Now under suspicion.'

'Yes. He knew Brandon?'

'They were at school together around here. There's a motive for you.'

Catherine drank her gin. The day had proved fruitful. Now there was a beautiful mid-afternoon breeze hitting the bar, a southerly coming up from the beach. Catherine suddenly longed to swim and wondered if she could get one in before the others arrived back.

Yvonne's drink was finished. She ran her finger up the side of the damp glass.

'Another?'

Yvonne shook her head. 'No. Long night coming up. I should be vaguely clear-headed, at least.'

'Never been a fan. The best thoughts come in sideways.'

'And the worst.'

'It's a chance I take.'

A man caught Catherine's eye as she walked down towards the beach. In a town full of colourful tourists, he was in dark shorts and a blue vest. He was tall and menacing. Even if you didn't know he had done time, you may have guessed from the poor artistry of his tattoos.

He exuded violence. It was in the way he held his head, two parts boxer, three parts bull. He had a bottle of mid-shelf bourbon in his hand. The bandage was still on his arm, the white discoloured by bodily fluids.

He noticed Catherine and kept walking towards her. A large family crossed the road to the beach, leaving Catherine and the lumbering, dark figure temporarily alone on the footpath.

She halted, forcing him either to avoid or pass her. The two gins she'd had bubbled in her guts as he moved towards her; then she felt a pulse of strength as this large, bearded man slowed his step.

'What do you want?' His voice was rough, and had a hint of echo, as if he were far away.

'Travis, I can help you. I don't think you killed Brandon. It doesn't fit.'

He breathed deeply. 'Yeah, but who are you?'

'I'm Catherine. I'm also someone who finds things out.' It could have been the gin talking, but hearing her own voice, Catherine believed herself. 'I found out about a photo of you smacking him at a rally.'

His eyes widened. Catherine's hands went to her hips. She kept talking. 'So you hated him, but I still don't think you stabbed him.'

'What do you know?'

'I know you would have stabbed him harder than the wound I saw.'

He stared at her. Catherine, who had been stared at by many a man, had never seen a gaze like this. It wasn't threatening; more sadly resigned. A vein pulsed in his forehead and his breathing was shallow. She could sense no alcohol on his breath.

Catherine had the sense that she had told him he was a ghost. A wrinkle in his face thickened and he snarled faintly and walked on.

Catherine didn't call out. Whatever thoughts he held, now held him completely.

Catherine watched his retreating figure as he crossed the road. The swallow tattoo on his neck dominated his side profile.

For the next ninety minutes, she forgot about Brandon Miles-Barclay and who had killed him. She forgot about by-elections and political rivalries. She forgot what time Britt said they would be home and who was supposed to be cooking dinner. She forgot about hats and fashion and how many days until the holiday was done. Catherine spent that time moving in the shallows, wearing her shorts and the bikini top she had used in lieu of a bra. She body surfed, she swam. She danced with children and their parents. She danced alone. She was aware that this was the moment she was living, and it was all she had.

A reformed alcoholic had once told her that people who only think of the past or the future were driven by ego and missing the point. The present was all, and sometimes when we dance in the waves, that natural playground, we can for a moment forget our own names.

The sun was still hot when she came out of the sea. For a while, she sat facing it, letting it dry her – she had brought no towel – and listened to the beach treble and the ocean bass that made this soundscape so very human and yet so much older than that. She checked her phone. No messages from Britt or Boris. She liked that. Not that they would have disapproved, or even have been surprised, that she went swimming instead of finding some form of research. Even so, it was nice to have a moment to herself that she didn't have to explain.

After twenty minutes, her hair was dry and her shorts acceptably damp for polite holiday company. Catherine made her way languidly along the beach and up to the path that would take her home through the dunes.

The roar of the beach became muted and augmented by the buzz of crickets and mosquitos. Catherine hadn't gone far when she heard a snapping of a dry branch behind her. She turned and glimpsed a shadowy figure disappear into the dunes. Catherine stood still, her fist curling. A couple came down from the opposite direction, smiling at her as they chatted. Catherine made room for them on the narrow path and walked slowly as they moved away. She watched them into the distance. After she had counted to thirty in Malay, she decided it was nothing and continued.

The figure reappeared after a few minutes, fifteen metres ahead of her, large and dark in the underbrush, away from the path.

Catherine's instinct was to move quickly. She hurried past and started running only when she was beyond him, straining to hear footfalls.

Nothing.

She turned at the mouth of the path that opened up to the road home.

Nothing. Just a family getting boogie boards out of a minivan.

With the family so close and one teenager taking an active interest in this deep-breathing woman, Catherine was emboldened to check the path again. Waiting for Golledge to jump out, stinking of herbs and bourbon.

Nothing. Just normal, average people, with dogs and children and lives. No boogeymen coming out of the dark to murder, or worse, bore her with non-sequiturs.

Up the road, she still felt uneasy. There was a line going through her head, muttered by Golledge days earlier. 'You have many lucky days.' There seemed to be a movement against this luck, and suddenly she wished the Glasgow Palace would appear in front of her, so she could move into its safe walls and drink a gin poured by Boris.

'No,' she said quietly. Surely, this was only some strange comedown from a good swim.

The tragedy of a swim is the same as that of life – it is temporary. Swims just feel more painful because the ocean does not change. She wiped the last of the salt from her eyes, again checking behind her. She saw a movement at a house a few hundred metres away, but nothing more. Once she crossed The Terrace, all seemed a bit more still.

By the time she was opening the door of the house, she wondered if she had imagined it. It could have been anyone under the trees. The shadowy figure was probably just someone's uncle darting back to the beach with a replacement soccer ball. Catherine poured an afternooner and chided herself on being spooked by nothing.

The house was beyond warm. One of the reasons it was cheap was it had no air conditioning. It was dark and almost sultry in the heat. Catherine considered going to Britt's room downstairs, where the house was at its coolest, but it wasn't much better, so she went to the back yard with her drink in hand.

She brought out her phone to call Boris. She scratched on the phone cover, thinking about feminism and whether it's a betrayal to want your burly best friend around. She decided that was even more ridiculous than anything else and dialled.

She sat on one of the outside chairs, watching the breeze push the eucalypt tree's branches around in slow circles. The phone rang four times before Britt answered Boris's phone.

'Hi.'

'How was cross bay hunting?'

'We got some good background, then the ferry wasn't leaving for an hour, so we stayed at the Sorrento pub for a while.'

'I hope you're not wanting to be chided. I have a gin in hand now; not my first.'

She was listening to Britt laugh as the first loud thump started. Catherine's hands jerked and she almost dropped the phone. She faintly heard Britt asking, 'What was that?'

In the back yard was an old steel gate, that Boris had established on their first night would not open.

The thump was something or someone smacking into that gate.

Catherine moved into a karate stance, dropping her gin, then realising the glass could have been a handy weapon. The gate crashed again. Catherine could hear Britt yelling through the phone on the ground.

As Travis Barker crashed through the gate, Catherine screamed.

11

All the connections on earth can't stop an ill-intended fist that's got lucky.

~ Britt Houden

He was hulking over her. Even from four metres away, sweating from exertion, drugs or something else. Catherine noted the wisps of grey through his dark beard and the deep lines in his face, and wondered why she noticed that detail when, really, she should be either running or stabbing. He stood square on to her, not advancing, yet. Catherine adjusted her own stance, seeking with her peripheral vision for things to block him with, and projectiles.

Fighting a bigger opponent, you went either long or close-quarters. Catherine wanted to keep it long for as extended a time as possible. At least, until some neighbours heard.

'No!' he yelled. The sound short and desperate. His stance went from fighter to frightened. He lowered his arms. He was breathing heavily and sweating. 'No.' he said more quietly.

Catherine heard a dog barking nearby. Barker returned to the broken gate and picked up something from beyond the fence. The bottle of bourbon.

Catherine didn't move, watching over her fight-ready hands, and painfully aware of the last time she did any combat training. He walked back on unsteady feet. His boots crunched over Catherine's broken gin glass.

The dog was still barking. Catherine wondered where the hell anyone else was. She'd screamed loud enough to break windows.

Barker sat down on Catherine's abandoned chair and unscrewed the top off the mostly gone bottle of bourbon. He looked up at her.

'I did it.' He said, and drank quickly. 'I killed the fairy.'

'You killed Miles-Barclay. That's what you're telling me?' Catherine's voice was even. She still hadn't moved from a fighting stance.

'Yep.' Barker looked her up and down. 'I scared you too, didn't I?' His face twisted cruelly. 'I bet you liked it.'

'Another minute and you would have fallen over.'

He threw the bottle, not hard, but hard enough. Catherine's hand whipped across her body and caught it. If she hadn't, it would have hit her face. Barker pouted.

Catherine sneered. 'Still a little scared aren't you, Travis?'

'Not of you. Not of anyone. Gimme the bottle.'

Catherine brought the bottle up like a club. 'Pick up my phone just there, Travis. Call 000 and pass it to me. Let's get the professionals involved and then we can have a talk.'

Then they heard the sirens.

'Cavalry's here, Catherine. May I please have a drink?' Barker's demeanour had gone to a blank politeness. Catherine thought of every prison cell she'd ever seen and threw him the bottle, gently.

In the past twelve minutes Boris had driven at mostly over 130 kilometres an hour, with Britt first on the phone to 000, then calling encouragement and reading the traffic. He'd run two red lights, overtaken a turning truck and honked as a large busload of Japanese tourists had taken space on the road for a group photo.

Ten per cent of Boris' mind was impressed by Andy, who hadn't murmured a single whimper for the entire drive; the other ninety was just trying to get to Catherine, in time.

He took the corner from Tuckfield Street into The Avenue on two wheels and powered down the street, braking slightly when he saw the flashing blue lights of the police car, then realising that didn't guarantee Catherine's safety. He brought the car up onto the kerb and somehow had the handbrake up and his seat belt off before the motor had stopped.

As fast as he was, Britt was faster. He followed her around the front of the house to the inexplicably open back gate. Nearby, a second police car was waiting. No ambulance. He pelted after Britt as she flew through the gate, running at Barker, who was in cuffs at the bottom of the garden. Police began to yell at them. Boris was shouting, 'Where's Catherine?' surprised how loud he sounded.

Two officers of different height and gender came towards him with hands up, no weapons. He couldn't look at them or hear what they were saying. He swung towards a movement at the back door.

Catherine stood there in the same clothes as this morning. Her hair was a mess. Boris ran to her.

It was only as he felt her in his arms that he started crying.

Britt watched as the police car pulled away, just as she had watched other cars drive on when she was the arresting detective. She should call Thomas or Perfetto to tell them, but she lingered. It was always a moment to savour, when someone was caught. It almost made up for all the times the murderer wasn't.

Britt sniffed the air and dialled Thomas' mobile.

'Houden. You want that drink?'

Britt closed her eyes. 'No drinks for you tonight, Luke. Travis Barker has just confessed to the murder.'

'To who. You?' he yelled. Britt could imagine his face turning red. It pleased her immensely.

'To Catherine. Then me.'

'Who's Catherine?' He was trying to keep his voice even. Not quite succeeding.

'A friend of mine. A milliner.'

'The nosey one Williams told me about?' Britt forced herself not to grin. 'That sounds like her, yes. Barker followed Catherine home, broke a gate and then confessed.'

'Why her?'

Here she had to tread carefully. 'She knew about the case. She's spoken to his daughter. I don't know, ask him. I'd give him a few hours though. He's three sheets.'

'Did you record the confession?'

'On my phone. I'll send it to you now.'

Thomas exhaled deeply. His disappointment was almost palpable. Britt smiled to herself. 'You're welcome, Detective.'

He grunted. 'I don't like how you've been involved. Neither will Williams.'

Britt put a little more cop in her voice. 'Thomas, I sent you the perp who's confessing, practically gift-wrapped. Are you really threatening me?'

'No, no. I just. I don't like it.'

'I didn't kill the guy. I just cuffed him. That's a first world problem you've got.'

'Yep. Thanks.' He rang off.

Britt breathed in as the sky began to turn crimson. If she'd had Perfetto's number, she would have called her first, then asked her to record Thomas' reaction.

At the end of the street, she could just see the foam of the distant waves. They were eternal, and in motion. For a second, she was still.

Inside, Catherine was telling the story to Andy as she sat on the floor in front of the couch, gin at her elbow. Boris sat closer to her than usual, while Andy lay on the opposite couch.

'I actually thought it was the other bloke, Golledge. Even though I'd seen Barker earlier today.'

'We saw him too,' said Andy lazily. 'He was about to assault someone. He was obviously getting something out of his system.'

Catherine grimaced. 'He did seem in two minds about going quietly tonight. He was like an animal getting in, then when he saw I wasn't going to go easily, he was all surrender. Then he threw a bottle at me.'

'What?' Boris was incredulous.

'Just playfully. Hard enough to hurt, soft enough not to be sent to solitary.' She grinned. 'I know enough to survive in H block.'

'Huh,' huffed Britt as she entered. 'You're not pretty enough.'

Catherine toasted her. 'You called the great Detective Thomas?'

'You'd think I had called the boss and taken credit for it. He gets to have his nice easy case and still complains. The man is a walking shit stain.'

Andy sat up on the couch to make room for Britt, who was sniffing the remains of the bourbon that Barker hadn't been allowed to take with him to prison. 'So, despite all the chat about seahorses, they had nothing to do with it?'

Catherine put her drink down. 'I don't think so, unless Barker was into poaching.'

'Did he mention why he killed him?' Britt called from the kitchen.

'He said he hadn't planned it. He was down on the beach and found someone he didn't like. That's all he said.'

Britt took a beer out of the fridge and one for Boris, who signalled thanks. 'Did you ask what he stabbed him with?'

'I really didn't have time. He'd barely got the confession out before the uniforms were here.'

Britt sat next to Andy. 'I wish I'd been here.' She sipped. 'I mean, obviously, because you could have been hurt. But I would have loved to ask a few questions.'

Andy burped. 'Example: did he stab your car?'

Boris reached for his beer. 'Was it him outside the house the other night?'

Catherine shrugged. 'Was it?'

'Could have been.' Boris took a contemplative sip. 'I guess so.'

'You don't sound convinced,' said Britt.

Andy stood up. 'None of you do. But the murderer has confessed, and we still have some time down here. I say we go to town and see what trouble we can get into.' He opened his arms, indicating the world was their oyster.

Catherine's eyebrows raised. 'Jesus, our adrenaline junky. They won't know you at work.'

Andy clapped his hands. 'It's prison, you see. It changes a man.'

Britt raised her beer. 'Let's hope so.' She finished what was left and stood. 'I'm in. It doesn't feel right yet, but perhaps an hour at the Zebra and all will be well. If you're up to it, Catherine?'

'All things considered, yes, but I would prefer the Glasgow Palace. Boris?'

'Tomorrow you go back to expendable, but tonight I'm sticking close.'

'Don't be silly, dear.' She put an arm around him. 'I'm indestructible. He didn't stand a chance.'

Two hours later Boris was wiping tears from his eyes as Andy tried to justify his love of salt on fruit. The move to the pub had proved a good one, and with the passing minutes, they were letting go of the many unanswered questions. More time was elapsing between the moments Boris looked across the room to see if Molly had materialised. Almost losing Catherine meant that, for a few seconds at a time, he could be in the moment.

He focused on Andy's voice. 'I know it's not normal, but banana and salt are my bag. Without salt, banana should not be consumed by anyone over the age of nine; but with salt, I'm telling you, it's a sophisticated and mature treat.' He gave them a knowing look and drank from his umpteenth pint of the evening.

Catherine leaned in. 'Andy,'

'Yes.'

'Friend.'

'Yes.'

'Sweet one.'

Andy replied, louder. 'Yes, Catherine, I am all ears for what you're are about to say.'

'Do you think it's wrong to want what you want?'

His forehead creased but he kept on. 'When it comes to salted banana, I am completely comfortable with my life choices.'

'Because a salted phallus as part of your daily routine could indicate you're repressing some complicated emotions.'

Britt almost fell on the floor. Andy rolled his eyes. 'I may seem repressed, as all Scots men are, but all that's happening at that time is potassium and sodium making love in my mouth.'

Britt cried out, choking with laughter. 'Stop, stop. I'm dying.'

Andy picked up the salt shaker and gave it a peck. Catherine and Boris both hit the table. Andy seemed about to go further when a waiter deftly took the salt and pepper shakers, and the tomato sauce, away from them.

Catherine kept laughing as they watched him go. 'You're not in Brunswick anymore. They don't tolerate those kinds of shenanigans here.'

Andy sat straighter. 'Ah yes. Dignity, always dignity.' He winked at Britt. 'You all right, hen?'

'I am. Just getting back to holiday mode.'

'Hmm,' came the collective murmur. They stared at their drinks. Jaunty hit songs from previous decades swirled around them.

Britt swirled her beer. 'I can't stop thinking that the wound doesn't fit the perpetrator.'

Catherine nodded. 'I found out today that Barker and Miles-Barclay both grew up around here. They've known each other for years. I don't buy the "I saw him on the beach and so I stabbed him" narrative.'

Britt put her drink down. 'But what about the Patriot's issue? Miles-

Barclay humiliated Barker. Maybe the other day was his first chance to get him back.'

'People have been killed for less,' Boris added.

Andy made a face. 'But he could have killed him any time, in a less public way. It seems even more stupid than your run-of-the-mill stupid.'

Britt's phone lit up. She stared at it long enough they could all see the name on it. Ken Williams. Head of Homicide squad. Britt's boss.

After three rings, Catherine offered to answer it. With horror Britt grabbed the phone and moved away from the table.

She took the phone out to the balcony. There was still a crowd out there, but Boris was sure she didn't mind who heard the conversation provided it wasn't Catherine.

Andy whispered. 'Have I met this mystery man?'

'You remember the angry old cop from that night at the Zoo?' asked Catherine

'Oh, him. How could I forget? I'd never heard such language from an Australian.'

'He's usually quite restrained. Almost gentlemanly.' Catherine sipped. 'Makes it worse, really. I imagine he's being extremely polite.'

Outside, Britt held the phone away from her ear and held onto the balcony. She wasn't shaking and didn't seem any less herself than a second ago, but Catherine knew the sobering effect that a call like that can have on you. She picked up her drink and went to Britt.

'How was that?'

Britt smiled, but it only worked on the bottom half of her face. 'Very polite. He even apologised for calling me while I'm on leave.'

'Hmm. Polite Williams. That's worse.'

'Yep. He was making sure I knew what was expected of me even outside working hours.'

'He would have much preferred you were in Thailand?'

'I'll make him pay next holiday.'

'Did he say anything specific?'

Britt shook her head. 'Only to enjoy my time and ensure that there were no complications with any investigations, ongoing or concluded.'

Catherine peered down at the street, suddenly wondering if Williams was doing surveillance. If so, he was doing it well. There was no sign of him.

'That about does it for me.'

'I knew you'd say that.'

Catherine gently grabbed her arm. 'You don't have to be involved.'

They both knew that point was moot.

There was a song on the stereo about heat that involved a heady saxophone. Catherine and Britt returned to the table. Britt took a long swallow of her drink. She looked at Boris and Andy, who fell silent.

'I don't even feel right if I'm ordered to feel right. This isn't finished.'

The next day, a banging on the door woke Boris. He passed the table, which was covered in teacups, beer bottles and the large notepad of possible plans: Find Raylene; back to BMB house; contact De Carle...

The knocking started up again. Boris called out, hoping to hell it was an early morning pizza delivery. He vaguely remembered muttering about it at about 4am and wondered if he'd sent an order that had just found him, almost seven hours later.

He opened the door, blinking and nauseous. Before him was Duc Nguyen, in shorts, looking as if he'd walked out of a men's health magazine. Duc stared at Boris as if he were a new type of mould.

'Hello?' Boris squinted against the light.

'Hi,' Duc began. 'You're Boris, right? Catherine's... friend?' The hesitation before "friend" happened from time to time. Catherine enjoyed that; it usually meant good things for her.

'Friend,' Boris agreed. 'Boris. You're Duc. Are you here to arrest me?'

Duc's brow creased, and he opened his arms wide, to display his lack of uniform. 'No. I was just here to see if Catherine had time today.'

Britt pushed in. Boris hadn't heard her coming. 'We've no plans today. Give Boris a second and he'll clean up some of last night's mess.'

'I will?' Then he remembered the notepad. 'Of course I will.' He disappeared up the stairs, adjusting his dressing gown.

Britt stood in the doorway, smiling and retightening the straps of her own robe. 'No work today?'

'No. The Sergeant gave me the morning off, something about needing a break from my face.'

'That's nice. The force doesn't change.'

'Well, they let people like you and me in now, but the language around the place, never.' Behind them, the sound of a glass shattering preceded a swear word from Boris. Duc looked back to Britt. 'Hey, I'm sorry. I'll come back. Let you guys wake up.'

Britt's hand closed over his upper arm. Duc allowed himself to be pulled in. 'It's okay. We just had a late night. Was there something in particular you wanted? Boris does good breakfast.'

'I don't know if you heard, but Barker was taken in last night, confessing. I don't buy it, but no one at the station wants to hear it. I thought maybe Catherine would. Or if you had any thoughts.'

'Come on up. We know all about it.'

Duc closed the door and followed Britt on the stairs. Britt called out, 'I'm coming up with Duc, Boris. Everything better look legal.'

Duc coughed. 'I really don't care if you have a bong up there.'

Britt's laugh was as light as feathers. 'Oh, good. I thought it could be a sting.'

When Catherine woke forty-five minutes later, she went to the living/dining room and swore an ancient Cambodian oath.

Duc waved at her. In front of him was a plate of eggs. Sitting across from him was Britt, also in breakfast mode. In the kitchen, Boris was flipping things in a pan.

'Why on earth is a handsome man here?' she demanded. 'I have decreed that no handsome man shall be tolerated in this house until I have had vast amounts of coffee.' Her hand stretched in a Shakespearian flourish. Her maroon robe, which was as tattered as it was beloved, shivered as she declaimed the injustice.

Duc grinned. 'I'm sorry to barge in, but for now I'm off duty and couldn't think of a better bunch of co-conspirators. Boris was very gracious to offer lunch.'

'And he's calling breakfast lunch? Disaster.' Catherine marched to the kitchen and lowered her voice. 'How could you let this happen?'

Boris looked at her, then at the two at the table. 'Early bird gets the worm.'

'Early mornings aren't my thing.'

'To be fair, it was half ten.'

'You're not helping, dear.' She indicated to the contents of the pan. 'Is that for me?'

'Yes, Catherine.'

Catherine poured a coffee from the stainless-steel jug and put the kettle on for her second, which she would need in a matter of seconds. With a look, she pleaded for Boris to help a damsel. Boris handed her a plate of eggs. She kissed his cheek and headed to the table.

Duc looked up. 'I knew Barker had confessed, but I didn't know it was to you.'

Catherine sat. 'I have a trusting face. People can't resist me.'

Britt blew on her tea. 'Hence the robe, to make it a fair fight.'

Catherine flicked a disdainful eyebrow at her.

Duc continued. 'So, you're okay then?'

'No, I have a hangover, which I blame entirely on Britt here. As to my encounter with Barker: pfft.' She gestured, the coffee having not kicked in sufficiently for full sentences.

Britt sipped her tea. 'Duc has the same doubts we do.'

'Really?'

Duc nodded. 'The knife wound, to start with. It's not deep or rough enough. Travis Barker is a hard man. He wouldn't even stab his food that softly. Or so I thought. He's suspected in a murder that was done almost as soft as a kiss.'

Britt grunted. 'Shivs don't kiss.'

'I know, and it was never proven, but it suggests he could do it.' Duc winced at his own contradictions. 'It still doesn't fit. Plus, I found out it wasn't even the wound that killed him.'

'Really?' Even through her foggy brain, Catherine knew her repartee wasn't up to scratch this morning.

'Miles-Barclay drowned, and he was high.'

Britt sniffed 'Coke?'

'MDMA.'

'Ahh' Britt nodded. 'The happy feel-good drug. That's why he went back into the water.'

'You suspected?' said Duc.

'I knew that wound wasn't fatal. It was well short of the left iliac artery. We've been wondering what makes a stabbed man go into the water, or keeps him there.'

Duc finished his toast. 'I'm glad I came here.' He suddenly stared across the room as if he'd been slapped. 'What?'

'Ah,' said Andy quietly, entering the room. 'Morning.'

12

The right place at the right time sounds great, until it refers to where the piano landed.
~ Andy McCafferty

The room went extremely quiet as Duc placed Andy with Catherine and Britt. They had, of course, met briefly at the Zebra three nights earlier, but Duc had been distracted then by drinks and hadn't made the connection.

'Andy McCafferty,' Duc said quietly.

'Guilty, officer.'

'The man who was just wandering past when I was chasing someone through Brandon Miles-Barclay's house two nights ago.'

'I really was just wandering past.'

'I know.' Duc said, rubbing his cheek. Catherine noted the lack of stubble. He thought handsomely, she decided.

'How do you know?' asked Britt. 'I mean, I know it wasn't him. But you sound like you know something else.'

'Footfalls in the garden indicated the break-in was done by someone bigger.'

Andy shrugged. 'I always thought I was tall.'

'I meant heavier.'

Then Boris turned up with a plate for Andy, his girth reflecting how comfortable he was in the kitchen.

'Oh, cheers, Boris. Sound man.' Andy brought his plate over to the table.

'Another tea, Duc?' Boris called from the kitchen, oblivious to the others watching Duc's face intently.

Duc breathed slowly in and out, then blinked twice. 'Love one, Boris. Thanks, mate, same again.'

Britt sipped her tea very deeply.

'Do you have any thoughts on it?' Catherine asked Duc.

'The break-in, or the murder?'

'The murder.'

Duc thought about it. 'I suspect it happened between nine and ten the night before, considering the discolouration of the corpse. Based on his clothes, he wasn't swimming. Also, I think he was with someone.'

Britt leaned in. 'Why do you say that?'

Catherine answered. 'MDMA is a social drug. I'm sure you could take it alone, but mostly it's a party or a date thing.'

'That was my thought,' said Duc. 'Maybe on the date thing too. In fact, one piece of evidence is CCTV footage of a woman running from the beach at about 10.35. The face couldn't be made out, but she was going hell for leather.'

Catherine grimaced. 'That would be consistent with the stab wound.'

'The other big thing for me – and I say for me because no one else is saying it – is the poaching thing. I was telling you about the seahorses issue the other night?'

'Yep, I looked into it,' said Britt.

'You did?' Duc was delighted.

'I did. Hai Ma, forty bucks a seahorse.'

At the sight of Britt and Duc smiling at each other, Catherine wanted to throw her coffee on them.

Duc kept going. 'Right. Not big business compared to drugs, but big enough that people are doing it.'

'How do you think it's related?'

'Don't you think it's interesting that one of the few politicians committed to a crackdown on it is killed a few weeks before the election?'

Catherine interjected. 'In which he was coming third.'

'I know. He wasn't going to be the local member, but he might have shaped the argument. Maybe he was on a date, but the poachers or the people behind them knew about it. Maybe they arranged the date. If you want to stab someone, MDMA is a great way to make it easy.'

'He'd have been happy even as he died,' Agreed Catherine.

Duc sipped his tea. 'It's all conjecture. I just know it almost certainly wasn't Barker.'

'Unless he was the date?' Britt said. 'I've heard from a few sources that Miles-Barclay had an active and varied sex life.'

'Yeah.' Duc nodded. 'I've heard that too. Only since he died. I was barely aware of him prior to the death.'

'Not political?' Catherine asked.

'Not to that extent. I look them up before election day.'

Britt blushed slightly. There was a silence.

'Can I ask something?' Andy had stayed mostly silent as he ploughed through his breakfast.

'Sure.'

'How do you feel about salt on fruit?'

Duc blinked. 'I find it actually enhances tomatoes, but aside from that I'm not a fan.'

'Cool.' Andy nodded. 'At least you're open to it.'

Half an hour later, Duc left with the promise of returning soon. As Andy did the washing up and Britt showered, Catherine loaded up the campaign website for Shelby Acland. After a page on her policies and three opportunities to either donate to the party or join, she found what she was looking for: a number for volunteer coordinator, Yvonne McSweeney. Catherine dialled the number.

'Yvonne McSweeney,' Yvonne answered.

'Yvonne, this is Catherine Kint. The milliner.'

Yvonne's voice sounded thick. 'And not a cop, from Brunswick. Hi. What's up?'

'I want to ask you some questions about the autopsy.'

'Can't now. At a thing. Call you in twenty–' she paused. –six minutes.'

'Thanks.'

'Vote for us.' She rang off. Catherine accepted the tea Boris brought her.

'Boris, what do you think of people who answer the phone by saying their own full name?'

Boris rotated his shoulders to crack his back. 'I love it. So cool, and you always know if you're talking to the right person. I'm a fan.'

'But you don't do it.'

'God, no. I'm not important enough. I would hate people to think I thought I was.'

'Bless ye, salt of the earth.'

'You don't do it either?'

'Not on telephone calls. I'll be Catherine, but I'm not going to give you everything straight away.' She raised her eyebrows. 'Buy me a drink first, sailor.'

Boris left the room, chuckling.

Catherine stretched out on the plaid couch. She picked up a newspaper and read an article about a diminished interest in the arts from students at primary school who saw merit only in science and mathematics as intellectual pursuits. Catherine was appalled. So would Leonardo da Vinci. Such thoughts pleased her.

She drank the tea and wondered about Green politics and the pitfalls of populism. How do you sell change to the comfortable, or how do you convince the people on the bottom of the heap that the best way to improve all our lives is higher taxes?

The reasons she didn't go into politics were similar to why she hadn't become a cop. Some jobs could take all the beauty and fun out of a life forever. She hoped Yvonne got the odd free lunch.

The phone rang.

'Yvonne. Thanks for calling back.'

'No problem. We're staging a die-in in Geelong today.'

'A what?'

'Three hundred green volunteers lying across Little Malop Street to signify that the Green's voices will not be silenced, even if you kill the candidate.'

'Are you making hay from the Patriots thing?'

'No. We can't even mention the suspect until after the trial.'

Catherine bit her lip. 'Of course. I knew that, but the die-in?'

'It's cheesy, but it's a good message and the other parties won't have the first story on the news. Shelby's polling is going up. There's even talk of coming second if we can eat enough progressive ALP voters.'

Catherine's eyebrows rose. 'That's a visual.'

'What did you want to ask about the autopsy?'

'Do you know much about it?'

'I'm entitled to as much information as you are, Catherine. I'm a political hack and you make hats. But yeah, I hear things. What do you want to know?'

'The MDMA thing. Why would he take that during a campaign?'

Yvonne was silent. Catherine wondered if she had gone too far. Yvonne had exactly nothing to gain talking to her.

'Yvonne? I'm sorry, but it doesn't make sense.'

'I know.' Yvonne's voice caught. Catherine reminded herself that to Yvonne, Brandon wasn't just a corpse and a mystery.

'Right. I'm going to ask: did he use drugs?'

Yvonne sighed. 'He was my friend, Catherine.'

'I know.'

After a moment, Yvonne spoke. 'He did, on occasion. It's one of the questions that's been going through my mind all night. Why would he use a drug, especially that drug, then? He had a full campaign schedule the next day. You can't do that with an ecstasy hangover.'

'Do you think he could have been drugged?'

'Possibly. Drugged, then stabbed. It doesn't fit with the suspect. The drug implies that he knew the assailant.'

Catherine rubbed her nose. 'Or had some tryst gone wrong?'

'I've been thinking on that, too. No way would he take drugs, but he was always up for some fun.'

'Do you know his schedule that night?'

'The night was free, one of the few. I was home. Everyone was. That's why the tryst thing is possible. But I can't think who. Who would he meet with?'

Catherine chewed her lip. 'What about Shelby?'

'What?'

'You told me yesterday they knew each other.'

'If you thought they were taking drugs together, you weren't listening.'

'Just a thought. She had something to gain.'

Yvonne laughed. 'Don't tell, friend. But I checked. She had a branch meeting. It's in the electronic diary we have in our email system.'

'Ah. OK. Not her then.'

Yvonne's breath was accelerating. She was walking. 'Yep, put that out of your mind. I have to go get her elected. Anything else?'

'Want to have a drink tonight?' Catherine hadn't been meaning to ask, but it came out.

'Possibly. We'll be swinging past Ocean Grove again today, then doing a function at Barwon Heads tonight.'

'Okay. That's not far. I'll find you in the sea of green.'

'See you then. Look forward to it.'

Catherine put down the phone, more confused than she was at the start of the call.

An hour later, Catherine and Boris were passing another "Keep Out" sign on the dunes near 11th beach. Assuming Miles-Barclay had been at the beach for a date, he may have been in the dunes: a well-trodden spot for rough romance, they had been told. Checking for clues wasn't the best idea on the 4am list of things to investigate, but it was the only one available. Boris hadn't been interested in playing Monopoly as an alternative.

What they were looking for physically, no one could say. Andy had suggested the flickering ghost of a seahorse that would whisper the mysteries to them. Britt and Catherine had ignored him. Boris was into it, mostly as the conversation had taken place at a late hour, when he was receptive to such things.

Boris pushed a branch away from his face. 'If they filmed our activities for a year, it would just be a montage of us going where we shouldn't.'

'Oh hush. We've done no breaking and entering at all in the past three months.'

'Aside from Thursday, when we broke in the Miles-Barclay's house?'

'Yes, aside from that. You've been too busy in domestic land. Plus, we only do it when there's a need.'

Boris groaned. 'Don't bring up Molly. I was having a Molly-thought-free day.'

Catherine stepped over a root. 'Is that why you were cooking everyone breakfast?'

Boris shimmied past two close shrubs. 'That and I woke up with hardly any hangover. That comes from the Great Spirit, and when it does, you must shower your friends with good fortune.'

Catherine scanned the sand and the trees. 'Whatever. The eggs were delicious.'

Boris stopped scanning to look at her. 'Are you okay? I noticed a shift in Duc's attention.'

Catherine looked down even as she ascended to the higher dunes. 'Ha. No thanks to you.'

He rolled his eyes. 'Oh, please.'

Her reproach was only half in jest. 'You could have woken me, or pretended to be Britt's ex or something. But no, you just invited him in and made them both tea. Duc probably thinks Britt has a servant.'

'People have thought that about you.'

'Yes, and it's never brought me the love and happiness I had hoped for. So, if Duc's like that, good riddance to his flawless facial features and better luck to the detective.'

Boris ducked a branch. 'No bitterness then.'

'No. May they have several beautiful mixed-race children who grow up to be activists and punk rockers.'

Boris laughed. 'You left out graffiti artists. But watch your mouth. Your kids may join the young Liberals.'

Catherine grabbed her guts. 'Not from this sacred womb, my dear. Ha. What's that?' In a clearing among the ti-trees stood the remnants of a small fire.

They looked around the site. Two empty cans of coke and a broken beer bottle were in the process of being swallowed by the sand. Boris pointed out a condom wrapper, and a few seconds later, the prophylactic itself. Catherine found a small mirror and a chip packet.

'You know what this means?' Catherine said, watching as he hunched near the ashes.

'Pretty much, absolutely–'

'Nothing.'

Boris nodded. 'This just means that people were here. If you could check the DNA, maybe there would be something to it, but it's a popular tourist destination.'

'And I imagine many of the said tourists enjoy coke, fire, and sex.'

'The three staples of the modern holiday diet.'

'Okay. Let's split up, give it another half hour and then head back to base. See if the actual police people in our contingent have any better ideas.'

'You mean Britt and Duc?' Boris waved a hand and headed east. 'If they've come back from their investigation.'

'Oh, I'm sure it's been a great exploration,' Catherine muttered.

The following hour revealed several variations on the first fireplace. People obviously came here, drank things, ate things. Sometimes they copulated and then left. At one stage, Catherine was vaguely intrigued by a nice cheese board that had been left out, but only because it was more expensive than the packets of salt and vinegar chip that were now bulging in her bag, which she now used to carry litter instead of evidence.

The day was cloudy but still hot. It was probably past midday and

Catherine wished she had brought some water. The whole "hydration is essential" phenomenon had passed her by. It irritated her that an entire generation needed security water bottles, like needy plants. Catherine drank only when she was thirsty, and, as she lived in metropolitan Australia, it was never hard to find clean water.

Fewer people were on the beach than yesterday. Catherine wondered what day it was, then, as she started back to the path, wondered about taking a swim if Duc and Britt were still playing detective.

She had gone further than she thought. It took seven minutes to get back to the path. When she reached the fence line, she felt the familiar and unwelcome sensation that she was being watched. She scanned both ways of the gravel track that separated the dunes. The hum of insects seemed to drop a decibel and there was a stillness in the air that she did not like at all. On either side, the path was deserted.

Catherine took a breath and slowly turned a three-hundred-and-sixty-degree spin, taking in every part of the view, wondering where the sensation was coming from.

She had decided that it was simply an echo of yesterday's experience, when a large figure appeared at the end of the path, one part stamping, two parts stalking. Shorts and a form of trench coat. Hair wild. Golledge. He was standing, watching.

Catherine brought out her phone and started walking.

'Had enough?'

'Where are you, Boris?'

Boris stood up from sitting in the shallows. 'I'm at the beach near 11th. What's happening? You've got the serious voice.'

'I'm being followed by Golledge. The weird one. Come up through the dunes and fall in behind him. I'll be walking past where we jumped the fence in about a minute.'

'Right.' Boris dropped the crab shell he'd been contemplating and ran. The tide was rising, so he didn't have far to go, but the dunes were almost vertical at that point. He jumped the wooden fence and ran up the wall of sand and scrub. His feet were hot inside his runners. He caught his cheek on a branch and swore. He touched his face, checked his fingers for blood. Nothing. Sometimes pain can disappoint us for a lack of results.

He kept moving. He jumped a root and came in close to the fence of the pathway. He could just see Catherine coming. He couldn't see anyone behind her, but she was still a way away. Boris tried to hide himself in the scrub and wished he hadn't worn the bright Hawaiian shirt that Molly had bought him for his birthday.

He pushed in behind the biggest trunk he could find, its yellow wood hardly a great camouflage against the bright orange of the shirt. He thought of taking it off. No. If he did that, Catherine would turn out to be a Police Patrol and he would be a large topless man hiding in the scrub waiting for someone to walk past. There are some clichés you never want to grow into.

He texted Britt to get to the beach path immediately. He switched his phone to silent, just in time as he saw Britt was calling. Boris pocketed the phone as Catherine walked past. She caught sight of him, pressed up to the trunk and rolled her eyes. Boris shrugged. Honestly, if she wanted a better henchman, they were around. They just cost more. Sometimes the ingratitude got to him.

He dropped the thought as Golledge moved past. He was shorter than Boris, but broader, and quite possibly mad by the way he was gibbering. That would make it hard to fight him if it came to it. Boris would rather square up to a sane biker than a crazy hothead. One knows the difference between surrender and oblivion. The other will keep punching until they feel better, which, when you're mentally ill, can take a long time.

'I'm behind,' he texted to Catherine, ignoring the two calls from Britt. He jumped the fence. Fifty metres behind Golledge. He could see the large man's hands, his fingers moving in a clutching motion. Boris wasn't sure if it was threatening or nervous. Either could meld into the other quickly. He wondered what Catherine had in mind, but suspected it was going to be aggressive. She would want to talk to Golledge: she loved transforming from prey to hunter.

Boris was momentarily distracted by the sound of two gulls passing above him. His attention returned to the two figures in front of him. Fifty metres apart from each other.

Just before the path met Wedge Street, Catherine turned decisively and strode towards Golledge with a small determined smile. It worked. Golledge immediately spun around and realised that Boris was behind him. Boris kept his hands in his pockets. He made eye contact but kept his expression neutral. Catherine could love the chase, but he didn't have to. What he did like was keeping people safe, and after yesterday, Boris had developed a feeling in his gut towards men who follow women.

He recognised the feeling as anger; not his usual emotion, but he was ready for anything. The part of his brain not focused on the moment was enjoying the feeling.

Golledge started mumbling to himself. His hands went to his head and then back down. He turned back to Catherine. She kept coming. Golledge hit panic point and jumped the fence to the dunes leading to the beach.

Catherine yelled. 'Golledge, hold it.' But he was gone.

Boris took off, jumping the fence and tacking towards Golledge as Catherine came from the other side. If they could get him before the beach, he would be able to talk. If he made it to the beach, they could take him but risked being seen and reported to the police.

Boris kept moving, even though he couldn't see Golledge anymore. He pushed through the sleepy leaves and branches of the underbrush. He caught a glimpse of black trench coat and pushed harder. He was sweating profusely, the sound of his own breath crashing through him. He figured that unless Golledge was fit, he would be struggling harder.

Abruptly, the density of the growth diminished towards the top of the dune and he could see the man, turned and panting, holding his side. A second later, Catherine came into view, looking more beach model than warrior woman in her denim shorts and white shirt. Still, she showed no fear. In fact, she was still smiling.

Golledge held his hands out in front of him. 'I don't hurt people,' he yelled.

'Good, don't.' Catherine called back. 'Why are you following me?'

'I don't hurt people.'

'I know, Golledge. But you've been thinking about it.'

Golledge reached into his coat and came out with an eight-inch knife. 'Not thinking, just want to be safe.'

Boris stopped moving forward, instead going sideways to get closer to Catherine.

Golledge's mouth was opening and shutting. He knelt down and reached into the sand at his feet. He took a handful of sand and lifted it to knee height before slowly letting it fall onto the ground again. He was singing under his breath.

Catherine kept talking. She was moving toward Boris as well.

'Okay Golledge. No one wants to bleed today. If you want to talk I'm right here. This is my friend Boris. We help people together. Can we help you?'

Golledge's neck wobbled as he spoke. 'Lucky people should help everyone else. You're a lucky one, Catherine. I tried to tell you that before.'

'I'm feeling lucky now, Golledge. Why did you want to talk to me? Did you want to talk, or something else?'

Boris winced. That was a misstep. If Golledge did want "something else", this wasn't the time to bring it to his attention. If Catherine agreed, she didn't acknowledge the mistake. She was close enough for Boris to touch. Golledge got another handful of sand and let it drop again.

'Sand's lucky sometimes.'

'Right. Why don't you put the knife down so we can talk about it?' Catherine started walking forward, Boris next to her. His mouth was dry. All he could see was the knife. He thought about Miles-Barclay and if it was the knife that had ended him.

'I don't think it's a good idea for you to be here anymore.' Golledge blinked a few times and a hard look took his mouth. His hand, holding the sand, moved slowly backward.

'Hey, Golledge, we don't want to hurt you.'

Another voice cut the scene. 'I'll bloody hurt you if you don't drop that fucking knife.' As she spoke, Britt came over the dune behind Golledge, with a black gun held two-handed.

Several things happened at once. The last few grains of sand fell to the ground as Golledge's knees buckled. He fell to the ground onto his back. Britt came further down the dune, walking sideways with her eyes looking down the gun sights. Behind her, Duc's head appeared. Still in civilian gear, but with a bag over his shoulder, jogging toward Golledge. Catherine pushed Boris gently back as they stood down.

Golledge was staring at the sky. When Britt got close, he put his arms up in the air, dropping the knife harmlessly to the ground. It rolled away from him.

'Hello, Sean.' Duc grabbed the big man and brought him easily to his feet. From behind his back, Duc brought out a pair of handcuffs and locked Golledge hands behind him. Golledge started singing again, but with tears in his eyes. Boris couldn't help but feel for him.

In forty-five seconds the big man was sitting underneath a tree. He was a good deal less threatening, especially compared to Barker.

13

Broken hearts, broken noses, broken careers. A good surf can fix any of them.

~ Duc Nguyen

Duc's bag had produced water, and everyone had a drink.

'So, who is this guy?' Britt asked Duc.

'This is Sean Golledge. He's a fisherman, a herb specialist, and a poacher. That fair, Sean?'

Golledge was staring straight ahead, shivering slightly despite the heat. He was sat down with the others standing around him. 'I don't hurt people, Duck.'

Britt's brow creased. 'Duck?'

Duc shrugged. 'It's Australia. If you think too much about a nickname, you're doing it wrong.'

He came back to Golledge. 'Sean gets in trouble every now and again. Sometimes he hears things. I've never known him to pull a knife.'

'I don't hurt people.' Golledge went into his mantra. His eyes were glazed.

'Sometimes he makes a lot of sense. Not today.'

'What did you want to talk to me about, Sean?' Catherine knelt down.

Golledge's wide face focused on her and he gave an idiot smile. 'You were closing in.'

'I was?'

'You're a lucky one. Anyone can see. That's why he follows you.' He nodded towards Boris. 'I knew when you woke me up that you would find all the pretty things. I know Duck's been looking for me.'

'I suspected Sean was taking a few things from the ocean. Seahorses and such.'

The big man stared at his cuffed hands. 'I have to. I have kids.'

'Where are they?' Catherine asked gently.

Golledge shook his. 'Three boys, all grown up. I still have to pay the mum. I have to.'

'Sean. Was that you in the car outside our house?'

'Yes. I had to check on you. Lucky ones find things. I did a little song for you, see?'

Britt asked, 'Did you put the screwdriver through my car?'

'I need to pay. I need to.'

'Pay what, child support?'

'That's it. Can you take the cuffs off?'

'He didn't actually threaten us,' Catherine told Duc.

Britt sniffed. 'He seemed bloody close to it.'

'I know. Now I'm not sure he ever was.'

Britt looked at Duc. 'Will you take him in?'

Duc took out his keys. 'The boss said if I do another off-duty arrest in plain clothes, he'll put me in a cell.'

'Sean, I'm Detective Britt Houden. I'll take the cuffs off, but there are lots of things I want to know. Do you understand?'

Golledge nodded.

'Let's go back home. All this will be better with tea and food.'

Andy had arrived home with things to make lunch just as they all walked in. He brought a plate of food and a pot of tea into the back yard, so they could sit in the fresh air. Britt let Sean eat first – he was hungry. She sat across from him.

'Did you know about the murder that happened here last week?'

'I was there.' He seemed more lucid now.

Catherine exchanged glances with Duc, who switched on a recording device on his phone. 'You were there. On the beach, last Wednesday?'

His face was motionless. 'Yep. I was there.'

'Did you hurt anyone that night?'

Sean's voice was soft. 'I don't hurt people.'

'Right, of course. Why don't you tell me what you saw?'

Sean breathed, momentarily distracted by a magpie flying past. 'I saw Barker. He's a bad dude. I saw him with a woman. They yelled a lot. I moved away for a bit, though I had to stay close.' He sniffed. 'Then I saw a woman, and I saw a man get stabbed. It was an accident that became real. He held his side, but he was still smiling. He talked to her. I didn't see the woman. I was too busy looking for Barker. I did see the dead man smiling. Then he walked into the waves. Silly.'

'Why were you watching for Barker?'

'He knows where the good ones are.'

'The good ones?'

'The horses. I don't know how he finds them, but he knows. I see where he goes. Also, I need to know where he is, so he doesn't hurt me. He doesn't let me find the good ones anymore. They're greedy now. Ever since he came back. Always taking. Never letting them grow.'

'Who's they?' Duc's voice was deep compared to Golledge's sing song babble.

'Other poachers, sometimes with Barker.'

'So Barker does poach?' Duc's eyebrow rose.

Golledge nodded before finishing his tea. He stared hard at the leaves at the bottom. 'There will be good ones tonight.'

Catherine asked, 'So, a woman stabbed Brandon?'

'Yes. A woman. First, a woman yelled at Barker. Then a woman stabbed the smiling man. You call him Brandon. I didn't know him. I don't know why she stabbed him.'

'You didn't see her face?'

'No. I watched the smiling man for a few minutes, because he walked into the sea. I was watching to see if Barker came back.'

Britt looked at Catherine. 'So, you saw the stabbing. And it wasn't Barker?'

Sean shook his head. 'Didn't see. Yelling. Then the smiling man went to the sea.'

Catherine's breathing slowed. 'I think we need to talk to Raylene again.'

'Yeah. I think so.' Britt nudged Duc. 'You want to do this by the book?'

He nodded. 'I'll make the call.'

Golledge was gone. A bargain was struck that Boris would get a full lesson in seahorses and all the tricks of a poacher, and in return Golledge could avoid the station. Britt thought about making him pay for the tyre, but didn't. After all, she had a job and her marbles, and he didn't.

Britt looked down at Duc from the sunroom into the garden. Duc was pacing, his phone pressed upon his right ear. She could tell how it was going. She had asked Duc not to push hard and not to mention her name. There was something in him that she liked. While he understood why she didn't want to rock the boat too hard, he himself didn't care. He was a real cop. He didn't need a rank of success to know it.

He held his phone away from his ear, as if the call was suddenly too loud. He didn't look upset; he was, in fact, serene through the apparent yelling. Then he hung up. Sensing her, he looked up to the window and shook his head. 'Okay,' she thought. 'We're on our own.'

She met him on the stairs.

Duc's voice was flat. 'They don't want to know about it. Anything that comes up is on us.'

Britt gripped the stair railings. 'Are you sure there's a connection between Barker's woman and the murder?'

'Sounds like it, but so far only from the mouth of a madman. I still think it's worth following up. Only thing is, I'm not sure it's the Raylene that Catherine was talking about. She and Barker have a daughter, but Raylene's in a de facto with another guy.'

'Who?'

'Jim Willow. Twice as tough as Barker.'

'Little rat faced bloke?'

'That's him. Not to be underestimated. I think he's even done murder. If you've heard his name, I'm not the only one.'

'We saw him the night you arrested Barker. They were drinking together.'

Duc bit his lip. 'Willow's high up in the Patriots movement.'

'A real charmer.'

'Yeah. Those guys just love Asians. And cops.' He opened his arms. 'Asian cops are their best friends.'

Britt kissed him lightly on the mouth. 'Have a good day at work.'

'You, too detective.'

Twenty minutes later, Catherine and Britt were walking to the town.

'I don't know what the plan is exactly,' said Britt. 'We push the mother of Barker's daughter to confess? Will that even work?'

Catherine was breezy. 'No, but we can try. I'm a big fan of trying things.'

'I'm not sure about this.'

'Which part? We have reason to think Barker didn't do it, which means the police have the wrong man. Maybe even the wrong gender.' Catherine halted abruptly. 'Gender.' She said under her breath. She grabbed Britt's shoulder. 'Try this on. You saw Golledge and Barker yesterday right?'

'Yep.'

'Golledge tells Barker the same thing he tells us, about seeing the woman murder Brandon. An hour later, I see Barker and mention the CCTV footage. Barker confesses to save Raylene.'

'His ex?' Most people want their ex in jail, not take the fall for them.'

'But they have a daughter together. Maybe he's protecting Kayla?'

Britt's nose wrinkled. 'It's not the stupidest thing I've heard.'

Catherine's phone started ringing.

'Yvonne, how are you, my friend?'

Yvonne sounded tired. 'I'm good. But I feel odd.'

With the sun on her skin, Catherine couldn't help being facetious. 'Well, you've barely slept in a few weeks and this time yesterday I watched you drink two pints of lager a half hour before going to work. That can catch up with you, I've heard.'

'Yep. Right. You remember I told you about the branch meeting that Shelby had the night Brandon was killed?'

Catherine nodded. She could feel Britt's eyes on her. 'Yes.'

Yvonne continued. 'I had a feeling. So, I checked it again. No location listed, no other attendees listed. I don't know exactly why but I feel there could be something in it.'

'As if the meeting didn't exist? An alibi?'

Britt was watching, trying hard to stay patient. Catherine had to admire her discipline. She would have snatched the phone by now.

'Maybe,' Yvonne went on. 'No, now that I say that out loud it seems stupid. It could have been with the Libs, or Labor about preferences; if so, then there's a reason for no details. I feel awful even saying it. Sorry. I'm being silly; too long awake.'

'Where are you now?'

'Ocean Grove. We're stopping here for a few hours' paperwork. The candidate is in Connewarre. She's doing a sit-down event at the community centre, talking to retirees about how their future grandchildren will be affected by climate change.'

Catherine had vaguely heard of Connewarre. 'Don't they mostly already have grandchildren?'

'Who will get skin cancer.' Yvonne was firm. 'If you start talking about people's grandchildren's grandchildren, the urgency gets watered down.'

'You did polling on this?'

Yvonne snorted sleepily. 'Don't ask how many hours I spent on that.'

Catherine wrote down a note. 'So, the candidate is alone?'

'The candidate, like all candidates, will not be alone again until election day. There's always someone with you. I'm just doing boring stuff. I'll be back with her at Barwon Heads tonight.'

'Right. Last question.'

'Yeah?'

'What's her policy on the poachers of seahorses and sea dragons?'

'She was asked one question about it and she gave a non-answer about the marine life of Port Phillip Bay being a great treasure, and she was looking to protect all of it. That issue died with Brandon. Why?'

'Probably nothing. I think we may all be tilting at windmills.'

'I'm with the Greens. It's practically our motto.'

'Translate that to Latin and I'll get a tattoo.'

Catherine hung up. 'Fancy a drive, Detective?'

'What are you thinking?'

Catherine rotated her neck, it gave a small crack. 'I want to scratch an itch, and I want to annoy a pollie.'

'And you want back-up for that?'

'No. I'm going to get thrown out. I want you to watch what happens afterwards. I'll explain on the way.'

Seventeen minutes' drive later, Britt walked into the community hall, which looked so much like every community hall in Australia that Catherine barely registered it, aside from a beautiful avenue of palm trees that led up to it. White weatherboards and a basketball ring on the side. Catherine wondered how many bored people had pushed a broom across it over the decades and where their bones lay. How much history had been seen by its broom cupboard?

It must be a special kind of a day for her to wonder such daft things. It occurred to her she was simply distracting herself from the next job.

She waited a full five minutes before walking in, and even then, she was worried that she and Britt would be the only people there under 55. She was wrong though; the hall was full of people of all generations.

Shelby was talking about the local primary school, recently closed, and the Greens' commitment to quality, local, state-run education. Catherine checked the candidate's accent and wondered if Shelby had gone to Geelong Grammar or College.

At a pause, Shelby's gaze moved across the room. Catherine called out quickly, 'Shelby.'

Shelby blinked, as if she recognised her. 'Yes?'

'Did you kill Brandon Miles-Barclay?'

More than a few people gasped. Shelby shuddered, then snarled. 'What?'

Catherine's voice was clear. 'It's a rumour that's growing on social media. I need to know.'

The atmosphere changed. People murmured angrily. Shelby sniffed. 'I've expected the question.' She raised her hands. 'It's okay everyone. She's allowed to ask.' She looked at Catherine, her face tight, her voice even. 'No. I did not. I loved working with Brandon and, like all of us, I am mourning. I find the question disgusting, but I did expect it. That is all.'

Catherine left. Two men at the door told her to go and jump. She smiled as she walked past the broom cupboard.

Catherine had walked the length of the town's main street twice before Britt emerged from the community hall. She passed houses, two churches, a fish and chip shop and a mechanic. Catherine knew from other small towns that she was seeing the polished part. Things always got dustier and more intriguing as you ventured further from the main road. Today, things were interesting enough on the main drag. Britt pulled up silently in the car. They didn't speak until they were 500 metres clear of town.

Catherine had been looking at Britt's face for most of those metres. 'What did she do?'

'She was uncomfortable. Took two more questions and then had a break. Went to the bathroom.'

'What's your read?'

Britt kept her eyes firmly on the road. 'I think there's something. Yet…' Britt counted on her fingers. 'She's in public, she lost a friend, someone just called her a murderer.'

'So, of course, she's uncomfortable. I don't doubt it.'

Britt geared down as they came to an intersection. 'She'd also prepared for the question. She wasn't shocked, but then she's a pro. A small town pro, but a pro.'

They drove past a huge poster of Kathryn Cambridge. 'I think that says more about the sensationalist nature of campaigns now.'

Britt sighed. 'We didn't learn much.'

'No, but I'm going to keep my eye on her. Don't you agree?'

'It's always hard to say. My gut says you're onto something. I hate that you did that.'

Catherine expected this. She let the silence go a few moments. 'Tabloid, huh?'

'Yeah, that whole "flush them out" thing. Journos do it. Good cops don't.'

'And you know what I'm going to say.'

'Yep, but I am a cop.' She cleared her throat. 'Enough of that. Let's get the boys involved.'

'Boris is with Golledge trying to get to the bottom of what he saw. What about Andy?'

'I think our Scots friend will look great in Green; can you make him a volunteer?'

Catherine brought out her phone. 'I'll call the coordinator.'

Half an hour later, Catherine went alone to the supermarket. She should have been getting eggs, milk and coffee, but she wasn't. Raylene was nowhere to be seen. Not in any of the aisles, and a further sweep of the car park was also fruitless. Catherine saw her looking at the roasted chickens and rushed over, only for the woman to turn around. Same hair; not Raylene. Catherine paced past the checkouts, and saw a figure walking fast outside the front doors, away from the Terrace. Raylene was still in her supermarket uniform, but had a bag with her.

Before Catherine was even through the supermarket doors, Raylene was approached by a young woman with dyed dark hair and goth makeup.

Catherine watched Kayla exchange words with her mother. After a few seconds, Raylene reached into her pocket and handed a note to Kayla, who smiled and walked away. Raylene started off again, double time.

Catherine counted four rows of parked cars between Raylene and her as she left the supermarket. Raylene powered through the spaces left by the cars inching around in search of parking. She was quick on her feet.

Catherine had to run to keep within fifty metres, wincing as she realised the band-aid had come off her blister. She grimaced as she followed Raylene towards Presidents Avenue, where she turned right. Catherine pulled her grey hat down further as she passed the police station; her scalp sweating in the heat of it.

A hundred metres later, Raylene turned left on the Avenue, just 400 metres west of the Catherine's holiday share-house. Catherine pushed to catch up. The undulating pathways were hurting her blistered foot. Throwing caution to the wind, she called out to Raylene.

Raylene turned, then saw Catherine, and walked faster, her feet stomping the ground and her head angled down.

'Oh, come on,' Catherine muttered. She hopped twice then started running. Within thirty agonising seconds, she had caught up. She ran on the nature strip beside Raylene to give her some space. 'For God's sake, I'm not going to hurt you.'

Raylene's head was still down, denying any eye contact. 'You're gonna get hurt if you don't piss off.'

'Do you really hurt people? Have you made a mistake?'

'I said piss off.'

'I can help you.'

Raylene was still looking down. They were passing smaller and smaller houses. Up ahead was an apartment block. 'I don't need help.'

'Then why not talk to me?'

'I've got somewhere to be.'

Catherine was keeping up, ignoring the pain on her ankle. 'Barker's gone. Who's left to be scared of? Is it Jim?'

Raylene's head snapped around. Catherine instinctively stepped back.

'You. Know. Nothing.' Raylene was breathing hard.

'Raylene, I can help you. You don't need to be afr–'

She stopped dead as Raylene brought a knife out. About the length of a long finger. Catherine's whole world became focused on the knife.

All sound disappeared as it sliced towards her waist, Raylene's centre of gravity now low. Catherine jumped back, blood rushing in her ears. If she hadn't, she would have been stabbed on the left side of the stomach.

Catherine moved to a crouch. 'So, you do know how to use those.'

Raylene went quick towards her, then stopped. 'You leave. You shut up, or you feel this.'

Catherine's voice was husky. 'You used one recently? Wednesday?'

Raylene's voice was low, she was sweating, but whatever she was scared of, it wasn't Catherine. 'I will gut you, bitch. I won't think about it. You run away, little girl.' She gestured right with the knife. Catherine backed away, arms wide.

'If you haven't killed anyone. You don't have to live like this.'

Raylene gestured again with the knife, but said nothing more. The knife disappeared as quickly as it had come, and she walked away.

Catherine let her go. She felt like crying, not because she was scared, but because moments like that proved that she should always be scared. Sure, she lived happy, but the universe was cruel, and people were awful, every single day.

She steadied her breathing as Raylene disappeared around a corner. When Catherine's day started, her biggest issue with Ocean Grove was loud fashion sense. Since then, she had been threatened twice with a knife. This town is like most humans: more dangerous than it seems.

She removed her shoes and felt the warm earth under her feet; she tasted the air, savouring it the way you can only do when you've had a brush with death, or you're newly in love. There was a salty overtone in the breeze and she wondered what more she could do before Duc or Boris had another idea.

The thought came to her again that perhaps she should just be on holidays. That thought built and said: meddling attracts annoying people and gets you closer to knives. Surely this is bad for your health.

'You look for one like that.' Golledge pointed out of the car window at what to Boris was like every other part of the water that stretched out towards the bay.

Boris squinted, keeping his hands on the steering wheel. 'Like what, mate? I can't see any difference.' They had left the road seven minutes earlier and were on a dusty track.

'Pull over.'

Boris obliged and Golledge took him down the water. There was little beach, just a small drop onto the waves.

Earlier, Golledge had shown him where the stabbing was, which told Boris very little, they had set out on the seahorse tutorial. After the fifteen minute drive, Boris felt he was right through the looking glass. Golledge had talked about magic before chatting about his boys, and how he had never paid child support until they were eighteen because he hated their mother and thought that when they were eighteen he would have his debts cleared. When Golledge had signed on for benefits, he found he owed twenty-five thousand dollars.

Golledge had always dabbled in poaching. It paid better than fishing and he didn't have to go as far out. Now he owed so much he wanted to do it all the time until his debts were done.

Boris heard the tale with a mix of pity and revulsion. That anyone wouldn't pay for their children out of spite made him realise how lonely some people could be.

Golledge pointed at the water. 'See how the water goes greenie-blue there?'

Boris raised a hand against the glare of the sun. He was only half sure he saw anything. 'Oh yeah.'

'And the waves are chopping in halves and halves there? That shows you where the seagrass is. You look for that, pop down and see what you see.'

'And take what you can.'

Sean blinked through his glasses, as if talking to a fool. 'Every horse is $40. Get ten and you've made it. Keep's you going and the magic working. Helps the boys too.'

Boris thought of what questions Britt would ask. 'Where do you sell them?'

He shook his ample head. 'There's a Chinese bloke in Geelong. He's a prick. Always pays.'

'Do you do it all year?'

'Little bit. Good stuff up around Lonsdale at the moment. The new boys are there every night. I can't go there. Since the bastards came up.'

Boris looked at him. 'Rivals?'

'Yeah. Stabby pricks. They don't like to share.' Golledge pushed his right arm forward. Boris could see a yellow scar; it would have been a deep cut.

Boris traced the line of it. 'How do they not get caught?'

'When you're in the water, you can keep a lookout.'

'You've got it all figured.'

Golledge smiled. 'Couldn't figure you. No magic could make you go.'

They stood there watching the waves. Boris gazed out to the horizon to see if he could still spot the difference when he looked back. He felt he could.

Boris looked again at Sean's arm. It had only just healed recently. 'Who are the new guys? Gangsters?'

'Flag wavers. But still do business with Asians.' He belched disapprovingly. 'The way they go on.'

'Patriots?'

'Yeah. Hate the Asians, and the blacks. Too much hate on them.' He loosed a high pitched giggle, then looked at Boris' tee shirt and hissed. He seemed in pain, then placed his hand on the left side of Boris' chest, muttering under his breath.

Boris felt hot, confused. He pushed against the big man and took a step back. 'What are you doing?'

Golledge was apologetic. 'You'll need that.'

'Get back in the car, you weirdo.'

Andy passed the leaflet out while smiling his most earnest smile. 'Save the planet. Vote Green,' he called, sure that this flyer would join many others in the bin at the surf lifesaving club. Thankfully, the council had given in to Greens lobbying and had installed a recycling service. In the sunshine, a steady throng of people came past, mostly ignoring the volunteers.

Andy had always called himself a centrist, only because he didn't really know much about the two sides of politics anywhere. Any time he forced himself to take notice, he saw people who were smarter and richer than him, not really answering whatever question they had been asked. It was the same in Australia as in Scotland, just with better weather.

Yet here he was, standing on a beach, wearing a Greens shirt and handing out flyers. Really, he was keeping an eye on the candidate.

Shelby should have been sweating in her loose white blouse and long pants, but she was at ease. Shaking hands and laughing easily. When required, she listened to people and nodded as they gave their points. Andy had been watching her for a half hour and was amazed at how hard she was working while making it seem easy. Perhaps he would get into politics just to watch them work. It was almost as interesting as the zoo.

'You'd give away bloody everything wouldn't you?' The voice was rasped and high. An aged man was pointing at Shelby, who returned the stare, her face neutral.

The man continued. 'People like me, born Australians, will lose everything because of you. You'll give it all away to whichever group you want to suck up to.'

Shelby stepped closer. 'I'm not sure I understand the statement.'

The man brought out, from his pocket, a small patch with the Australian flag on it. 'What would you do for this? How hard would you fight for this?'

Andy moved closer, aware of others moving away.

Shelby's face softened. 'You served?'

The man straightened. 'I did.'

'Thank you.'

The man blinked. 'What?'

'I said thank you. I can't thank you enough for fighting for this country.'

The man's voice squeaked as he answered. 'Would you?'

'I already am. This place is changing. I think you'd agree. I want to protect it.' As she spoke, a burly volunteer approached the man, who was now only a foot from the candidate. Shelby held up a hand. 'I'm fine, Ben. This man's entitled to ask questions.'

The old soldier had brought up a handkerchief to his eye, voice breaking as he spoke. 'I hear what you want to change and it makes me worry you don't care for what happened before. To us.'

Shelby placed a hand on his shoulder, lightly. 'You fought. We're fighting. Your fighting was harder, but ours is just as important. We can agree that we love this place.'

The man sniffed. He handed the patch to Shelby. 'You keep this.'

'Thank you. What's your name?'

'Warren.'

'Warren.' She spoke so softly Andy could barely hear it. 'I will keep this forever. Thank you.'

14

Progress is made by wading through muck, and looking like you know the way out.
~ Shelby Acland

Britt smiled as she answered her phone. She had just spoken to Catherine about Raylene, and was hoping to speak to Duc, and now he was calling her.

'You're not supposed to use your mobile while on duty.'

'Ah yes. There's the issue. I'm not on duty.'

'You only started an hour ago.'

'I was thirty minutes into patrol when I got called in and told I'm on annual leave for the next week and a half,' Duc said drily. 'They want me to clear my head.'

'Oh shit. Forced holiday.'

'I guess they don't want me muddying the waters while they build the case against Barker. I can't believe it. There's a leave ban on because of the tourists and they're pushing me off.'

'Sorry, Duc. Want to find me? I'm on the beach.'

He paused, and Britt felt her stomach start to contract. Then he spoke, sounding happier. 'I was hoping you'd say that. Both things.'

'11th Beach. Bring your togs. A swim will clear your head.'

Two hours later, the four Melbournites and the police officer from Ocean Grove sat around a table in the back yard of the rented house. Boris was beginning to wonder if it were possible he was getting sick of fish and chips. Andy had insisted on them, citing it as a possible last supper for the disciples, and then he had paid, so no one was complaining.

Catherine chewed meditatively, then said, 'There's three possibilities. The murder has something to do with the poaching and we watch that. The murder is political, and we watch that. Or the murder has nothing to do with either and we're wasting our time and getting Duc closer to a reprimand.'

Duc waved a potato cake at her. 'My mum would love someone to blame for my lack of career progression, but it's mostly me.'

Britt nudged him. 'You sound way too proud of that.'

He smiled. 'The political and the poaching could be linked. Miles-Barclay campaigned on the seahorse trade. I'm sure if I got the poachers in an interview room, I could find out how much they knew about him.'

'What about Acland?' Catherine asked.

'Don't think so.' Andy answered before Duc could speak. 'She's the real deal. She cares about the place and the world. I don't think she'd be into murder, or poaching for that matter.'

'She's benefitted a good deal from the murder. She's gone from nobody to national profile in a week.'

Duc accepted this. 'Someone was going to. Yes, she benefitted, but the money the Patriots are generating through poaching alone. I think we need to move on this. Plus, Acland has a clean rap sheet. You should see the size of the Patriots'.'

Britt exhaled. 'Duc, has anyone ever called you bloody-minded?'

'Most people I've met.' He winked at her.

Catherine gestured with a chip. 'What about the woman connection? The stab wound was done by someone small, at least someone weaker than Barker. I haven't seen any small Patriots.'

'That's what got me pushed out today. I pulled the file on Raylene. She's got form with a knife.'

'Doesn't she just?' Catherine grumbled while contemplating another calamari ring. 'Has she got another job?'

Duc poured some vinegar on his chips. 'I suspect that Raylene may be part of the poaching operation. She was there on the night.'

Catherine blinked. 'She mentioned something about me not interfering with their work. I didn't think she meant the supermarket.'

Andy's brow creased. 'Why would Barker have confessed then?'

'I think he's protecting Raylene,' Duc said softly.

'Who's his ex,' Britt said.

Catherine put down her glass. 'He could be protecting Kayla. She's young and needs her mum.'

'Especially with Jim Willow in the house.' Duc wiped his mouth. 'Willow and Barker were inside together. Willow has all the power in that friendship. Perhaps that's why Willow is able to work with Barker but live with Raylene.'

Britt nodded. 'Okay. You've got me convinced. Let's get the poachers tonight and see where it goes. Boris, are you in?'

'I'm in. Andy?'

'I'm for surveiling the Greens, only because it seems less likely we'll be killed.'

Duc motioned to Catherine. 'I know it's not where your gut is taking you, but we need all of us for my plan to work. You and Andy on the boat. Britt and Boris in the water. I'm on land with a badge and a gun. They're not looking to the bay for an investigation.'

'Where are the Water Police?' Catherine asked.

'Underfunded, working the boat show in Geelong, and not taking my calls.'

Catherine leaned back. She thought again of what might have happened on that Wednesday night. She could see Miles-Barclay on the beach. Blood pouring from his side before he walked into the waves. Why would the Patriots drug him before stabbing him?

She took in the group, all eyes on her. This was why she liked working with Boris alone. She brought a chip to her mouth and caught sight of her watch. Five thirty-five. That was one thing she had, for once. Catherine Kint had time. 'Okay let's find the poachers. I'm not convinced, but I don't have a theory to counter it.'

Duc smiled, visibly relieved. Catherine saw Britt squeeze his hand under the table. He winced slightly as he asked, 'So, how much experience do you guys have with motor boats?'

The roar of the boat was exhilarating. Britt expertly geared past the breakers and then around the peninsula. Catherine looked left to the beach as the spray wet her face, the undulating dunes and in the distance the Point Lonsdale lighthouse. She turned back to Andy beside her, equally exhilarated in a life vest that matched hers. Boris grunted behind them as he tried to get his wetsuit to fit: they had found it in the house's garage and it was snug, to say the least.

'Nice boat,' she called to Britt.

'Yeah. Duc didn't seem the boat-owning type.' She shrugged. 'I'm not complaining.'

'And he trusts you to drive it while he stays on land with a badge. Well played, Houden.'

Andy nudged Boris, yelling. 'When was the last time you went snorkelling?'

'Two months ago. Molly took me to Magnetic Island.' He shrugged, palms up. 'Turns out I'm good at it.'

Andy's eyebrows lifted. 'Hidden depths everywhere.'

After fifteen minutes, they were coming into Point Lonsdale. Britt, scanning for rocks, powered the engine down. There were a few other boats in the water, and two hundred metres away they could clearly see people on the rock pools, tourists and locals. Sharing ice cream and playing beach cricket.

A familiar red Holden was in the car park. Catherine couldn't see inside the car, but imagined Duc sitting inside, or not far away. Watching them.

Her phone buzzed. A text from Duc. 'I see you too. Aussie boat is here.' Cute.

Boris stood in the boat, bracing his legs to not overbalance. He pointed to a space three hundred metres away, further from the lighthouse and beach. 'There.'

'What do you see?'

Boris kept pointing, amazed that he could spot it so easily. 'Seagrass. That's where the horses will be. That's where the poachers would be.'

Britt manoeuvred over to the patch. A boat with no one in it was anchored about two hundred metres away. It sported two Australian flags.

'I suspect the doctor is in.'

They drove the boat in a slow circle around the grass reef. One snorkeller surfaced, then another a few metres away.

Boris pointed them out. 'I see snorkels.'

Britt spat into her mask. 'This is too easy.'

'We knew where they'd be here,' Catherine said. 'Now to convince them to go back to shore and into the waiting arms of the constabulary.'

'Lucky I'm so charming. Wouldn't you say, dear?'

With that, she tipped backwards into the sea. Boris smiled at Catherine, who understood she was being mimicked.

'Sincerest form of flattery,' he said before he put in the mouthpiece and also tipped off.

Four months ago, Boris would have been terrified of this. The water pushed in on him as he swam, all motion adding to the dense sounds that filled his ears. He eased through the bubbles and kept Britt's flippers in view as the seagrass came closer. A huge undersea cluster ebbing and flowing with the waves, seemingly a live creature with one brain. Boris moved sideways, following Britt and saw the staccato surges of a pot-bellied seahorse. He almost laughed with delight, forgetting that he was about to go toe to toe with poachers. The horse sensed him and retreated to the deeper grass.

Boris became aware of two figures, as large as him, about fifteen metres away. One grabbed something and placed it in a bag.

For the second time in as many days, Boris got angry. The seagrass was like a paradise, and thieving from it for money was almost sacrilegious.

Boris shadowed Britt as she moved closer to the poachers. She closed in, tapping one and motioning towards the shore with her badge. The poacher, a short person, spun in the water and kicked away, flippers pushing bubbles towards Britt. Boris lost sight of the other diver for a second, but saw Britt swimming after them.

Boris broke the water, then caught sight of the poachers, four boat lengths away, before they both dived towards their own boat, moored fifty metres away.

Boris went after them, kicking hard as the water darkened. He tried to calm his breathing through the snorkel.

He chased the larger of the two. His arms were starting to ache, but he pushed harder. The poachers' boat loomed closer and Boris sensed the distance between them growing. Unthinking, he kicked harder, holding his breath, his heart thumping loud in his ears.

The diver was more experienced than him and fitter. Soon, Boris had to break the chase and come up for air. He dived again and saw the man two boat lengths away. Beside him, Britt was struggling with the other diver, whose bag fell away. The bag spilled a half dozen seahorses, who charged away to the grass like an undersea cavalry.

Boris let out a cheer through his snorkel and then kept on at the other man. He surged through the water, ignoring how ragged his breath was getting. The man was closing in on the boat. Boris was gaining, though, and with a last surge, he grabbed the poacher's finned foot. The foot kicked back at him, catching his shoulder. Boris grunted and grabbed again, shoving the man's face above water.

'Police,' He panted, amazed at his own lie. 'Get to fucking shore. You're done.' He sucked in air like a hoover even as he yelled.

The diver dropped his hand to his side. Boris got close instinctively, pressing his advantage, but the man suddenly swiped at him. Boris tried to catch his arm, then gasped at a thin pressure against his chest; and then the sting.

He never even saw the knife, just the blood that filled the water as the man pulled himself into the boat.

Catherine missed the moment her friend was slashed in the water. It was Andy who yelled "blood" and made her swing around. She knew it was Boris, even from the boat, she cursed herself, as if it wouldn't have happened if she'd been paying attention; if she hadn't been distracted by the young men playing soccer on the foreshore. With Duc into Britt, Catherine was easily distractible. Focus returned as Boris yelled.

Catherine ran through several scenarios in her head but there was nothing she could do. She hated it, and did the same as anyone powerless: she called someone. She called Duc.

He picked up instantly. 'I see blood.'

'I think its Boris.' One of the poachers was swimming away from the blood and towards his boat.

'Shit. I knew they should have taken the guns.'

'Britt's not like that. She thought the badge would work.'

'Can you get to them?'

'I've never used a boat. Can you talk me through it?'

Duc tried to be calm. 'Break, throttle, steer with the tiller. No wait. I see them. They're coming to land. I'm gonna get them.' He rang off.

Catherine gripped the boat. 'Andy, what do you see?'

Andy had his binoculars practically pinned to his eyes. 'If Boris is the one cut, then Britt is helping him to shore. One of the poachers is in the boat and the other's almost there. I can't see any sharks.'

'What?'

'Blood in the water, brings sharks.'

'Jesus Christ, Andy!' She hit him, not hard. 'A problem shared is not a problem halved.'

He gaped at her. 'Sorry.' He put his binoculars back up. She followed suit, view now fixed on the boat moored a hundred metres away.

The first poacher was hauling his mate into their boat. It was twice the size of Duc's, which admittedly was smaller than most four-person tents. One poacher started up their engine; the other threw down a bag and ripped off their flippers. The first one, still masked, brought up the anchor. The other gave Catherine and Andy the finger. Catherine was sure the latter was a woman, and quietly gave Duc a point.

Andy's attention had been drawn elsewhere. 'They've made it to the beach. Boris is being held up by Duc. He got a towel. He looks alright. Jesus, you can see the blood following him in, though.'

Catherine watched the boat with the two Australian flags move away.

Someone had cut Boris and she was watching them move through binoculars. This didn't suit her worldview at all. She threw the specs down and turned to Andy.

'Break, throttle, steer in reverse because it's a boat. How hard can it be?'

'No, Catherine. You can't. This will be the end of us.'

Catherine was on her haunches staring at the motor. 'Nonsense, man. I was damn close to dux at school. I can work this out.'

Andy spoke at full volume. 'It will be the end. Of at least one of us. Probably me.'

'Throttle, throttle'. She took in the various parts of the engine. 'I can do it, Andy.'

He sat down and gripped the sides of the boat. Catherine could have seen the whites of his knuckles, but she was paying no mind. She pulled up the anchor, turned the keys and hit the throttle.

The Scotsman roared as if in pain as the boat heaved. Backward. Catherine killed the engine and burped quietly. 'Okay, that's reverse, Andy. You ready?'

'What about Boris?'

'He'd want me to catch the bastards. Ole!' The engine roared and the boat bucked, rushing forward this time. Catherine whooped and tightened her grip on the tiller. A quiet part of her head took a personal inventory. Yes, Boris was hurt, but he wasn't dead. Yes, the poachers knew how to drive their boat better than her, but she was moving. Yes, she didn't know how to slow the boat down, but in a chase, that's okay.

A bump pushed them up as they knocked an underwater rock. Andy said nothing. It was the most stoic she'd ever seen him. She refocused her attention on the boat she was chasing. They had moved closer to shore, where Catherine didn't want to go. The rock had rattled her, and she could see the lump it had made in the steel. That was tomorrow's issue.

As she took what felt like an outside lane, she kept the tiller in hand. This felt easy, like driving a car against beautiful expanses of roads. Andy, it seemed, was starting to trust her more, and even seemed to be enjoying himself. 'We're gaining on them, Catherine.'

'Sure are. Just keep your thinking cap on.'

Andy looked back, his hair slick with water from the surf. 'What do you mean?'

'Well, I'm following them, right?'

Andy held onto the side, his face a picture of exasperation. 'Well yes, we both are.'

Catherine kept her eyes straight ahead. 'Any idea what we do when we catch them? They have knives.'

'Oh sh–'

Then they both heard a bang.

Catherine's mouth twisted bitterly as something brushed her life vest.

'Oh, they've got a gun too.'

Duc was reversing out of the car park while trying to keep his mind quiet. Boris' wetsuit was soaked in blood, with people running at him as he came up to the beach. Duc and Britt had pulled him up to the car and only now was Britt able to start pulling his wetsuit off. Duc knew the University Hospital in Geelong was thirty-seven minutes' drive with no traffic. He knew that a man can bleed out in less than three minutes. He knew Boris had been cut seven minutes earlier in water. This was the extent of what he knew and it played on repeat in his head. He gunned for the Bellarine Highway.

In the back seat, Britt's voice was firm. 'I'm pressing down, Boris. It'll hurt but I need to stop the blood flow.'

'Ahh.'

'How's that?'

His voice was cracked. 'That hurts, keep going.'

'You're doing great, mate. You're going to be fine.'

Boris let out some shallow breaths. 'This is horrid. I can't stop thinking of Molly.'

'That's okay.'

'She doesn't love me.'

Britt kept her hands firm on the wound. 'Her loss mate. She's…'

Duc couldn't stay silent. 'What is it, Britt?' He said again, louder. 'Britt?'

Britt saw Duc's eyes wide in the rear-view mirror.

Boris coughed. 'What is it? Britt.' His voice wasn't pleading, but it was close.

Britt looked, wide eyed down at his chest. 'I think you're all right.'

'What?'

'You've had a knife slice to your left pec, but only by a few millimetres. That's the only cut. You're bleeding, but you're okay.'

'Pec,' howled Duc. He started laughing, a high-pitched, hyena laugh. 'Oh shit.'

Boris looked down. Seeing the cut in his left man-boob, he almost whooped. He clamped the soaking towel down on it and joined the laughter. Duc pulled off the road, quivering. He turned, unbuckling his seat belt.

'Oh, shit, brother.' He was panting. 'I thought I'd killed you. Hey.' He scrambled inside the glove box. 'I've got some heavy-duty band-aids. Let's get you sealed up.' He started laughing again, with a chorus from the back seat.

Britt shook her head. 'We should get him to hospital anyway.'

Boris raised a hand. 'No, let's check in with Catherine. I want to be sure she's okay. Pass me that, man.' He reached for the bandages. 'I can do it myself.'

Britt's phone started ringing. 'Catherine. He's all right. It's just a scratch.'

Boris watched Britt's face pale. 'You what?'

There was a bang that Boris could hear from the phone. Britt looked at Duc. 'She's chasing them. They're going back to Ocean Grove. They have a gun. Go!'

15

You should only be in a hurry once a year, maybe twice.
Hurries make you miss the good things.

~ Sean Golledge

Catherine threw the phone to Andy so that she could focus on steering. After the first bullet, she had veered out towards the bay and in doing so, worked out that by pulling a lever on the engine she could lower the speed below warp ten. For a horrible moment she thought the hunter might turn prey and the poachers would chase them, but they seemed content to be making a getaway.

A sentence Golledge had said earlier in the day was replaying in her mind: 'An accident became real.' Catherine checked her life jacket and the small chunk missing where the bullet had passed her. Andy paled, but she focused on steering while he crouched low and spoke on the phone.

Catherine had called Britt to check on Boris. Once she knew he was okay, she'd got excited about it and revved the engine. The poachers had shot again, this time going nowhere near them. Now she listened to Andy on the phone to Duc.

'I don't know,' he said twice. Yes. We're going towards the setting sun. I have no bloody idea where we are compared to Lake Victoria because–' he shouted, '–we're in a boat! Not a helicopter!'

Catherine suppressed a giggle. She kept her eye on the poachers in the boat, one was driving, but when she got too close he turned, drawing his gun. Catherine immediately pulled back.

The other diver was talking to him. They were yelling. The driver lashed out with the gun hand, the other fell, arms splayed against the floor of the boat. Catherine inhaled sharply, thinking they might fall overboard. They didn't, but stayed at the back of the boat, as far from the driver as possible.

'I don't know why she's doing it,' said Andy. 'We have no idea what to do if they stop. Yes, still going to the west. I can see the bridge in the distance. Yes, possibly. What on earth are you guys going to be able to do from the freeway? Call the bloody coast guard!'

With the spray in her eyes, Catherine focused on the bridge. It meant going over the waves, which took more nerve than Andy had; not that he had a choice.

She knew that bridge; they'd driven over it coming in. Barwon Heads. Where the Greens function would be on. Maybe Catherine could have that drink with Yvonne anyway, if she wasn't deafened by Andy's shrieking by then. Or dead...

Duc was driving with his phone on his ear.

'Mate. You're doing fantastic. I know cops of ten years who can't keep this cool.' He held the phone away from his ear as Andy kept cool at an even higher volume.

'Andy. I know you're too far away to get shot. If you've got them in the channel, then you can hang back. Britt's called the cops already. They're going to be waiting at the beach. They're going to be able to stop them.'

He swung past the Ocean Grove caravan parks. There were flashes of green and red shirts throughout them, even a police car, but Duc's eyes were firmly on the road. Boris had pulled his wetsuit back on and was resting his hand on his left breast.

Britt craned to see the bridge coming up. 'Slow when you get on it.'

Duc swore. 'They just fired again.'

'You got your sidearm?'

'It's at the station.'

'Where's your spare?'

Duc grimaced, keeping his eyes on the road as he pulled open the glovebox and pulled out a false top. A revolver dropped into his hand. He passed it to her. 'Don't tell.'

'Don't worry, cowboy, I know your type. Slow when you get to the bridge.'

'You're not going to shoot from the bridge. This is my town.'

'Of course not. Just slow down.' She reached into the glovebox and took out a standard evidence bag. Not to be found in citizens cars or, officially, in officer's cars. She took a look at Duc, at the sweat running down his face.

Why did she always fall for bad boys?

The bridge came into view. She could see two boats coming up the heads. The closest flew two flags from the back. In another two hundred metres, a shooter would have access to roughly 1000 tourists.

'Slow it down now.' She said, unbuckling her seat belt.

Duc slowed the car to a crawl. 'What are you thinking?'

'No time, baby.'

She jumped out of the car, rolling to save her bare feet. In three steps she came close to the edge. Half her head screamed: what are you thinking? A calm voice answered: about Williams not approving. Of Dad. Of Andy.

She leapt to the bridge railing and pushed up. As she jumped, all she could think was how much her mum had always hated Catherine. Then she heard a loud bang, which didn't come from her gun.

As Britt jumped off the bridge Catherine heard her voice, Andy's voice and a gunshot. Britt hit the water, without any tell-tale jerking. Catherine steered the boat closer and felt around for something to throw. Finding nothing aside from Andy, who was as pale as the sand on the shoreline fifty metres away, Catherine scanned the water for her friend. She was aware that the two poachers in front of her were doing the same.

A flash came up on the other side of the poachers' boat. A pale maiden, rising from the water like something from King Arthur's legends. Then the rasp of two shots ringing out and the poacher's boat's engine was silenced.

The foundered boat drifted sideways; the larger diver jumped into the water with a bag in his hands.

Catherine gunned the engine, only to hear it whine and fail. She looked at it, not sure where the petrol gauge would show her an empty tank.

The shots were good. Smoke rose from the engine. Britt kept her gun in the air, kicking to stay afloat.

'Hands up.'

A woman's face appeared over the side of the boat, a purple bruise coming up over her right eye.

Britt masked her surprise. 'Police. Where's your mate?'

'Gone.'

Britt kept the gun towards the boat. 'Where's the gun?'

'Gone.'

'You Raylene?'

She scowled. Nodded.

'Knife?'

Raylene threw it to the far end of the boat, then placed her hands on the stern. Britt grabbed the boat and pulled herself in single-handed. It was empty aside from Raylene, who glared at her, then spat over the side.

'Knife was only ever for him, anyway,' she said.

On the shore, Britt could see the blue lights flashing.

Boris watched the shore from behind Duc. Three officers and at least thirty onlookers were there. As the boat came slowly in, he could easily make out Britt and one of the poachers.

Duc's head craned urgently. 'Where's the other one?'

Boris's phone went off in his pocket. Catherine…

'Hi.' She spoke urgently. 'The other one's jumped in, probably swimming north.'

'You mean out to sea?'

Duc looked at Boris sharply.

'No, dear.' Catherine sing-songed. 'Try again.'

Boris's face reddened. 'Oh right. Duc.' He pointed. About six hundred metres along, a dark shape in the water was swimming upstream and out of sight.

'Let's go.' Duc ran back to the car.

In the car, Duc turned the key. 'I think I know where he's headed. I found something up here about six months ago that I thought was odd, like a way station. There were two sets of eskies chained to a tree.'

'Don't you want back-up?'

'If the Sergeant even knows I'm here, I'm toast. This is you and me, mate.'

'Okay. Hope he doesn't have a gun still.'

'Me too. My girlfriend stole mine.' Duc cackled as they drove up the river. 'I doubt any gun could work after being submerged that long.'

They came to a stop. The light was fading, quicker in the shaded part of the Barwon River. It was a peaceful place, with lush trees covering the river and paths of beaten dirt stomped down by generations of fishermen.

Duc killed the engine and got out. Boris stood beside him, his chest hurting. He wished he had his boots.

Duc walked out towards the water, baton in his hand. Aside from ripples from the current, it was still. 'It was somewhere near here. Let's split up. Slow walk a hundred metres each way, then back.'

'Right.'

Duc paused, raising his chin. 'Hey, take this.' He handed over the baton.

'Thanks.' Boris took it and exhaled low.

The light was playing against the brown water of the river as Boris moved along the bank. He became aware of birdsong as he went, easing into each footstep to save the soles of his feet, which hadn't quite toughened up after a week at the beach. The cut on his chest throbbed. He could hear his heartbeat in his ears. The earthy smell of the water came to him and he thought about how peaceful this would be on a different day. He heard a far-off bump and turned, trying to find Duc in the dappled light. He couldn't see him, but heard no other signs of a struggle.

Boris stepped over a fallen root and wondered how many steps a hundred metres was and whether he should have started counting. He checked the water as he walked. He heard, but didn't see the leaves part as someone came out of the underbrush, and felt a sharp pain in his right shin. He yelled as he fell on the dusty path.

Boris rolled forward and onto his back, lashing out with a foot and catching his assailant in the face.

The man staggered back. Boris jumped to his feet, his shin throbbing. With the mask off, Boris recognised the rat-faced Jim Willow. He was crouched with a long knife in his left hand.

'Cut you once, bitch tits.' Willow's voice was gravelly and low. He came closer, gesturing with his right hand. 'One last shot, fat boy. I'm gonna gut you quietly.'

Boris pulled back, playing for time and hoping for Duc, but Willow had him hard against the river. He was about to jump in when Willow darted in from the right. Boris sidled left, stepping over a root and seizing a branch to bring down on Willow's head. As the small man ducked, Boris took a swing with the baton, just missing Willow's shoulder.

'That's it, fat boy. I'll take you.' In the dusk, Willow's face was a mask of wrinkles and a grin that wouldn't leave. The smile was twisted, worn by a man that forgot what fear was.

Boris hated that grin. He knew this man would kill him and enjoy it.

He must have blinked Willow saw it and came charging, his knife high and arcing down with the acceleration. Boris went to parry with the baton, missed. He tried to move so the knife would hit something other than his face. He closed his eyes.

The sound of Duc's shoulder hitting Willow was just audible over the whipped dog noise Boris made.

Willow crashed into the undergrowth, swearing. A second later he was on his feet, but Boris had recovered and took him from the side with a right hook.

Willow staggered, dropping the knife and Boris had him pinned with an arm behind his back a second later.

'Jim Willow.' Duc's voice was low. 'You're fucking done.'

Willow spat blood at Duc, still trying to get away from Boris. 'Go back to where you came from, Gook.'

Duc slipped handcuffs on him and grabbed his rat's tail. 'I'm from Geelong, shithead.'

16

Do you ever look at the stars and wonder if you're seeing the dying embers of a once bright universe?

~ Boris Shakhovskoy

Catherine had just been pulled ashore by a handsome young officer with a bald head and a nice smile when Britt approached her. In the twenty minutes since all the shooting Catherine had called Boris and Duc more than eight times each, getting nothing.

Britt, covered by a grey towel, embraced her. 'Duc got him, half a k upriver. He and Boris are bringing him down now. It was Jim Willow.'

'I thought so. Was the other one Raylene?'

'Yep. She's pretty beat up.'

'Okay. Is Boris all right?'

'A little bruised and he'll have another scar, but he's fine.' Britt waved to Andy who was being pulled off a police boat, as puffed up as a bantam cock.

A crowd was coming from the Barwon Heads Tavern to have a look, a mix of corporate attire and green shirts. Catherine scanned the crowd for Yvonne. She spotted her, then followed Yvonne's gaze back over Catherine's shoulder – to a dark-haired woman carrying a bag over the Barwon Heads Bridge.

A candidate, alone.

Catherine's head was suddenly quiet. She thought of a drugged man smiling as he drowned. She thought of a meeting with no details. She imagined a knife that would leave a splayed wound.

Under her breath, she murmured. 'An accident became real.'

The possible scene solidified in her head, and for a second, she thought about Miles-Barclay's stab wound. Her head cocked, then very slowly, she stood up and gripped Britt's arm.

'You won't need the confession, Detective.'

Catherine ran towards the bridge, through the park and past the kids play equipment. Andy was at her heels, and she wondered if he had come to the same conclusion. Britt called out, metres behind them both.

Shelby Acland was moving fast across the Barwon Heads Bridge. It took a full minute for Catherine to catch her. In that minute, she watched Shelby search inside her bag for something as she glanced towards the still police lights below.

'Shelby!' Catherine yelled. Shelby turned and screamed. She walked backwards three paces, her mouth working, then sank to her knees.

'No,' she almost sobbed. Catherine could see she was on the edge. 'Not you.'

Catherine slowed, but kept coming forward. 'You're running away from a scene that everyone else is interested in, with a bag that you won't let go of. What's in the bag, Shelby? What are you so desperate to get rid of?'

Shelby clutched the bag to her chest, then started to throw it.

'Shelby. My Scots companion here is a celebrated diver.' Catherine broke eye contact for a microsecond to make sure Andy was with her. Britt was a step behind, her hand on Andy's arm, pulling him back. Catherine continued. 'You throw that, you're confirming your guilt. It's a knife, isn't it? Not a knife for stabbing. It was an accident, wasn't it?'

Shelby squealed louder. 'No.' Then more quietly, 'No.'

Yvonne's voice called out. Catherine turned to see her running towards them, a uniform beside her.

'Catherine, what the hell?'

'It was an accident, Yvonne,' Catherine told her. 'Shelby didn't mean to stab him. She didn't even bring the knife. He did. I don't know all of it, but I know she stabbed him. Inside that bag, she's got the knife.'

Shelby Acland stared imperiously. 'That is ridiculous. How dare you?'

Britt brought out her badge. 'You didn't sound at all like that a second ago. Britt Houden, Homicide.' For the briefest of seconds, her eyes met Catherine's. Then she turned to the uniform. 'Constable, take that bag, please?'

With a yelp, Shelby fell to her knees and dropped the bag. Yvonne and the uniform looked at each other, and Yvonne nodded. Shelby kicked out and pushed herself against the bridge railings. She was crying now, freely but quietly.

Catherine ran forward, snatched the bag and tossed it to the uniform. He upended it. Inside were several files, a notepad, and a cheese knife with a splayed tip.

A second later, Britt and the officer held Yvonne McSweeney back as she screamed words that would never be fit for parliament, though there was no question of sanctions against her. One phrase was repeated over and over.

'I fucking *knew*.'

17

I occasionally feel the ocean is sneering at me.
Then I remember its indifference, and the sneering seems good.

~ Andy McCafferty

'Branch meeting, huh?' Britt poured another wine for herself. Duc put a hand over his glass when she moved to fill his.

'Got to work tomorrow. Could be a big day.'

Andy pushed his glass in. 'I'll have his. Come on. Spill the rest of it, Nguyen.' They were alone in the open-air part of the Zebra bar on a Tuesday night, with the tourist season finally coming to an end. Duc checked around the bar and kept his voice low.

'Miles-Barclay wanted to meet with her. Smooth things over leading into the campaign. Shelby had a plan to discredit him, so while he laid out the trout and cheese, she slipped MDMA into his champagne.' He looked up. 'Maybe just a little more after all. Thanks Britt.' He ignored Britt fondly rolling her eyes as she topped up his glass. 'After a while, he starts yabbering and she knows he's getting high. She turns on her recording device and starts asking about the bullying allegations. He confesses he leaked them, but only because he loves her and because he loves the party.'

Boris picked up his beer. 'So, he was quite high.'

'Yeah. Must have been. So, Shelby gets the blackmail tape she wants, but then he talks about using her temper to change the world. Her passion and such.'

Catherine put her glass down. 'Then Shelby got mad?'

'Yep. To hear him give all the beautiful reasons for why he ruined her, it was too much, and she took the knife from the board and pushed it into his side.'

Britt exhaled noisily. 'That'll kill the mood.'

'Not with that much MDMA on board. He looked at the wound and said, oh, of course, you're mad. And you're right. I've gone too far. Don't worry. I'll go swimming and you can have the election. You can have it, Shelby. I can change the world later, he said. Right now, I'm going to go swimming.'

Duc left it there, and took a long sip.

'Far out.' Boris shook his head. 'I'm never taking drugs again. How did you guess, Catherine?'

'Y'know. I think I was led to it.'

Boris' baulked. 'What?'

'Yvonne. Everything she told me led to that moment, making the accusation she couldn't make. Consciously or not, she played me. Beautifully.'

Britt's voice wavered. 'Do you think Yvonne was involved?'

'No. I just... I'm not sure how much she knew or suspected.' Catherine sucked her cheek in contemplation. 'When Raylene pulled the knife on me that day, I think I knew it wasn't her. This murder was done by someone who hadn't stabbed before. I just couldn't pick how it happened. Then I saw Shelby running away when everyone else was looking and I knew she had the knife, I think she wanted to keep it. Yvonne had said she was a hoarder.'

Boris burped. 'You can imagine her smiling for years as she served the Premier cheese with that knife.'

Andy whistled. 'Hell of a guess. What was the story about Raylene running from the beach?'

Duc shrugged. 'Acland might be the type to tell, but Raylene wouldn't say a word.'

'I think I know about that.' Catherine sipped her drink. 'Raylene was terrified every time I spoke to her. I suspect she had been seeing Barker on the sly, but he was getting scared too and broke it off that night. When Golledge told him he'd seen a woman, Barker panicked that Raylene was about to go to prison. Then when I talked about the woman, it confirmed his fear. He confessed so she would stay free.

Plus he was terrified of Willow too. I suspect that burn on Barker's arm came from Jim.'

'He was burned, but wouldn't say anything about it,' Duc agreed. 'Well, in three months Raylene will be free. Barker got out today. I'm surprised I haven't seen him. You make a lot of assumptions, Catherine. Good ones, but assumptions.'

'That's the beauty of not being a cop. Anytime I'm wrong I just make more hats.'

Duc got up to leave. Britt held out a hand. 'Stay, it's our last night here.'

'I really have to go. I have a meeting with the Senior Sergeant tomorrow. It's one of the good meetings. I hope.'

'Okay.'

'You could come see my place, though.'

Britt toyed with her glass, then drained it and stood. She threw keys to Catherine. 'Don't wait up.'

Andy, Boris and Catherine laughed. Andy got up to buy another round.

Boris took a long breath. 'Good holiday, Catherine. I haven't thought about Molly all day.'

Catherine put a hand on his shoulder. 'Good. Hey, look.'

Down on the street, outside the fish and chip shop, a large man and a teenage girl walked out with an armful of paper parcels. They walked close, without touching. Boris couldn't see them from here, but he knew the man had some of the worst tattoos he had ever seen.

Two weeks later. Boris and Catherine were together again in their natural surroundings: Catherine's lounge room with Boris on the couch, Minty the cat on his shoulder and Catherine sitting on the floor in front of the coffee table.

Unusually for them, the television was on. Spilling the news of the Australian Labour Party winning South Barwon by a swing of four per cent. The second story of the night was of Yvonne McSweeney, who after Shelby Acland dropped out due to her arrest, had managed to spearhead the greens campaign, taking fourteen per cent of votes, even though they would not be counted under Victorian law. Thus making her an impressive "non candidate" which would certainly be noticed by the party executive.

One of the pundits quipped Oscar Wilde, stating that for the Greens to lose one candidate was a tragedy, but to lose two was just careless.

'She's given so much,' Boris noted. 'Yet now, she'll be a punchline in Australian political history.'

Catherine stretched. 'Or she could be seen as the candidate that rose when all the others fell. I'm not surprised she got fourteen per cent, but she still lost. Defeat, Boris. It's a trial, but it's beautiful. And in defeat lies the true romance of life. Any fool can look good in victory. It's the unloved, the lonely, the unaccepted and yet courageous, that are the true wonders of our small planet.'

'That sounds like us.' He held out his hand, she took it, and for a moment they sat, contently watching the commentary.

Until one of them felt deeply uncomfortable and let go and awkwardly suggested, 'Um, pizza then?'

ACKNOWLEDGEMENTS

This story starts with a difficult meeting I had with Annie Hall from Threekookaburras Publishing in March 2016. Annie was justifiably unimpressed by an early version of Pachyderm and had bought me a drink to soften the blow. In the conversation she talked about seahorse poaching and said there could be a book in it. It started a spark, and on my birthday in 2017 I opened a new notebook which titled 'Coastal.'

Andrew Hall, a marine biologist told me all about seahorses, and I thank Bella Cunningham for making that connection.

I had great support from the Victorian Electoral Commission and the Greens regarding their processes around elections. A particular thanks to Marian Smedley who was very generous with her time regarding the recent political history of South Barwon. Robert Larocca pointed me to some of the more colourful misadventures in southern politics and is continually generous with research and time.

Mick Hearn (Doctor Mick to you) gave great advice after reading an early draft and is always a great source of wisdom (paired well with Guinness).

My friend Duc Nguyen, who runs two excellent Music venues in Vietnam, was appalled that I used his name and demanded the character be killed off on page 3, it is with the greatest respect that I defied him.

Louise Kent and Adam Palmer both stepped into the 'world' with me – which is hard to do and it's very comforting to be able to talk about the work with someone who talks back (outside of your head). Their guidance and brilliance made the work possible.

Sean Golledge is a friend of mine who has been a huge support to my other books. His cameo got out of control, (always a sign of things going well, as a novelist you don't so much build a house as light a fire).

Now to my current Publishing home! Lindy Cameron took on my book and the two previous after Threekookaburras shut its doors in 2019. Lindy is a powerhouse of support for local crime authors and deserves full-throated gratitude from many – which now includes me.

Narrelle Harris edited the work and gave me a masterclass in extraneous words and why no one needs them unless they're funny.

A tip of the cap to Andrew Nette who has been a great support and introduced me to some of the coolest people in fiction.

I'd love to thank the 1000s of friends who support me, but we'd run out of pages (yes, I'm that lucky). Special shout out to the people who I've waffled to about this project way too late on a Thursday night. You know who you are.

This book is dedicated to my parents, who did everything I needed to have a good time on this planet. I owe them something special, they got this instead. They'll understand, they're parents.

Anytime I need a big brother I go to my little one.

My kids remain my biggest helpers, they tell me what works and what doesn't. Eliza knows humour like Catherine knows hats, and Cormac's laughter is the perfect collision of joy and mischief.

Louise is still the person I want to share a hammock with forever. She is generous, fierce and makes me choke with laughter at least weekly.

AUTHOR'S NOTE

Ocean Grove is a real place, full of wonderful people. The dastardly deeds in this book say more about the author's imagination than the actual town.

HUGH McGINLAY

Hugh is a writer, musician and optimist. Now three books into the Catherine Kint series, he continues to be amazed at the levels his imaginary friends have been accepted into other people's heads and bookshelves. As a musician he has released four albums and occasionally gets played on the radio. He lives with his wife, two children and various animals in Melbourne.

www.ingramcontent.com/pod-product-compliance
Lightning Source LLC
Chambersburg PA
CBHW020652260626
47157CB00008B/3007